FRENCH LEAVE

Anna Gavalda

FRENCH LEAVE

Translated from the French
by Alison Anderson

Europa
editions

Europa Editions
214 West 29th Street
New York, N.Y. 10001
www.europaeditions.com
info@europaeditions.com

Library of Congress Cataloging in Publication Data is available
ISBN 978-1-60945-511-8

Gavalda, Anna
French Leave

Book design by Emanuele Ragnisco
www.mekkanografici.com

Cover illustration by Mariachiara Di Giorgio

Prepress by Grafica Punto Print – Rome

Printed in the USA

FRENCH LEAVE

W ith one buttock in space and my hand still on the car door, I hadn't even had time to sit down and already my sister-in-law was nagging me: "For heaven's sake . . . didn't you hear the horn? We've been here for ten minutes!"

"Good morning," I answered.

My brother turned around. A little wink.

"You okay, sweetheart?"

"I'm good."

"You want me to put your things in the trunk?"

"No, thanks. All I have is this little bag, and my dress . . . I'll stick it up back."

"Is that your dress?" she asked, raising an eyebrow at the ball of chiffon on my lap.

"Yes."

"What . . . what is it?"

"A sari."

"I see . . . "

"No, you don't see," I corrected her gently, "you'll see when I put it on."

Was that a grimace?

"Can we get going?" asked my brother.

"Yes. I mean, no . . . Can you stop off at the corner store, there's something I need to get . . . "

My sister-in-law sighed.

"Now what do you need?"

"Some depilatory cream."

"And you get that at the corner store?"

"Oh, I get everything from Rashid! Absolutely everything!"

She didn't believe me.

"All set, now? Can we go?"

"Yes."

"Aren't you going to fasten your seat belt?"

"No."

"Why don't you fasten it?"

"Claustrophobia," I replied.

And before she could start in on her refrain about transplants and the horrors of public hospitals, I added, "Besides, I want to sleep a little. I'm exhausted."

My brother smiled.

"Did you just get up?"

"I never went to bed," I explained, yawning.

Which was a patent lie, of course. I'd slept for a few hours. But I said it to annoy my sister-in-law. And I was right on target, bingo. That's what I like about her: I'm always right on target.

"Where were you this time?" she grumbled, rolling her eyes to the sky.

"At home."

"You threw a party?"

"No, I was playing cards."

"Playing cards?!"

"Yes. Poker."

She shook her head. Not too hard, though. Wouldn't want to muss the blow-dry.

"How much did you lose?" asked my brother, amused.

"Nothing. This time I won."

Deafening silence.

"Might we ask how much?" she relented, adjusting her designer shades.

"Three thousand."

"Three thousand! Three thousand what?"

"Well . . . Euros," I said, acting naïve, "rubles wouldn't be much use, now, would they . . . "

I chuckled as I curled up. I had just given my little Carine something to chew on for the rest of the trip.

I could hear the cogs turning in her brain: Three thousand Euros . . . click click click click . . . How many dry shampoos and aspirin tablets would she have to sell to earn three thousand Euros?... click click click click . . . Not to mention employee benefits, and business tax, and local taxes, and her lease, subtract the VAT . . . How many times did she have to put on her white coat to earn three thousand Euros? And the Social Security . . . add eight, take away two . . . and paid vacation . . . makes ten, multiply by three . . . click click click . . .

Yes. I was chuckling. Lulled by the purr of their sedan,

my nose buried in the fold of my arm and my legs tucked up under my chin. I was pretty proud of myself, because my sister-in-law, she's a piece of work.

My sister-in-law Carine studied pharmacy, but she'd rather you said medicine, so she's a pharmacist, and she has a drugstore, but she'd rather you called it a pharmacy.

She likes to complain about her bookkeeping just when it's time for dessert, and she wears a surgeon's blouse buttoned up to her chin with a thermal adhesive label where her name is stitched between two blue caduceus logos. These days she sells mostly firming creams for buttocks and carotene capsules because that's what brings in the most cash; she likes to say that she has "optimized her non-med sector."

My sister-in-law Carine is fairly predictable.

When we heard about our stroke of luck—that we were about to have a purveyor of anti-wrinkle creams in our own family, a licensed Clinique vendor and Guerlain reseller—my sister Lola and I jumped up on her like little puppies. Oh! What a warm welcome we had in store for her that day! We promised that from then on we would always go to her for our shopping, and we were even willing to call her *Doctor* or *Professor* Lariot-Molinoux so we'd be in her good books.

We'd even take the suburban train just to go out to see her! That's really a big deal for Lola and me, to take the train all the way out to Poissy.

We suffer physically whenever we're dragged past the Boulevards des Maréchaux.

But there was no need to go out there, because she took us by the arm at the end of that first Sunday dinner and confessed, lowering her eyes, "You know . . . uh . . . I can't give you any discount because . . . uh . . . if I start with you, after that . . . well, you understand . . . after that I . . . after that you don't know where it will end, do you?"

"Not even a teeny tiny percentage?" replied Lola with a laugh, "Not even any samples?"

"Oh, yes . . . yes, samples, yes. No problem."

And when Carine left that day, clinging to our brother so he wouldn't fly away, Lola grumbled to me as she blew kisses all the while from the balcony, "She can stick her samples you-know-where."

I totally agreed with her, and we shook out the tablecloth, and changed the subject.

Now we like to ride her about all that. Every time we see her, I tell her about my friend Sandrine, who is a flight attendant, and about the discounts she can get us at the duty-free.

For example:

"Hey, Carine . . . Give me a price for Estée Lauder's Double Exfoliating Nitrogen Generator with Vitamin B12."

You should see our Carine, lost in thought. She concentrates, closes her eyes, thinks of her list, calculates her margin, deducts the taxes, and eventually goes: "Forty-five?"

I turn to Lola: "Do you remember how much you paid?"

"Hmm . . . Sorry? What are you talking about?"

"Estée Lauder's Double Exfoliating Nitrogen Generator with Vitamin B12, the one Sandrine brought back for you the other day?"

"What about it?"

"How much did you pay?"

"Gosh, how do you expect me to remember . . . around twenty Euros, I think . . . "

Carine repeats what she said, choking on her words: "Twenty Euros! Estée Lauder's D-E-N-G with Vitamin B12! Are you sure about that?"

"I think so . . . "

"I'm sorry, but at that price, it's got to be a counterfeit! What a shame, girls, you've been taken for a ride . . . They put Nivea in a counterfeit jar and no one's the wiser. I hate to tell you," she insists, triumphant, "but your cream is rubbish. Absolute rubbish!"

Lola looks absolutely devastated: "Are you sure?"

"Ab-so-lutely sure. I know what the production costs are, after all! They only use essential oils at Estée—"

This is where I turn to my sister and say, "You don't happen to have it with you, do you?"

"Have what?"

"The cream . . . "

"No, I don't think so . . . Oh, yes! I just might . . . Wait, let me look in my bag."

She comes back with a jar and hands it to the expert.

Said expert puts on her half-moon glasses and inspects the offending item from every angle. We watch her in silence, waiting with bated breath, vaguely uneasy.

"Well, Doctor?" ventures Lola.

"Yes, yes, it's Estée Lauder all right . . . I recognize the smell . . . and the texture . . . Lauder has a very special texture. It's incredible . . . how much did you say you paid? Twenty Euros? That's incredible," sighs Carine, putting her glasses back in their case, and the case back in her Biotherm pouch, and the Biotherm pouch back in her Tod's handbag. "That's incredible . . . at that level, it's cost price. How do they expect the rest of us to survive if they undercut prices like that? That's unfair practice. No more,

no less. It's . . . there's no more margin so, they . . . It's downright disgusting. It saddens me, you know . . . "

Carine is plunged into an abyss of perplexity. She turns
to her cup for consolation, stirs her sugarless sugar into a
coffee without caffeine.

After that, the hardest part is to keep our cool as far as
the kitchen, but when we finally get there, we begin cack-
ling like turkey hens in heat. If our mother happens to go
by, she says despairingly, "You two can be so nasty . . . " and
Lola replies, offended, "Uh . . . excuse me? I actually paid
seventy-two Euros for that piece of shit!" And we burst out
laughing again, holding our ribs above the dishwasher.

"Well that's good, with everything you won last night
you'll be able to contribute to the gas, for once . . . "

"Gas AND toll," I said, rubbing my nose.

I couldn't see her, but I could sense her smug little
smile and both hands placed nice and flat on her knees
squeezed tight.

I raised my hips to pull a big note out of my jeans pocket.

"Put that away," said my brother.

Up she piped: "But, uh . . . really Simon, I don't see
why—"

"I said put it away," my brother said, without raising his
voice.

She opened her mouth, closed it, wriggled a little,
opened her mouth again, dusted off her thigh, touched her
sapphire, put it straight, inspected her nails, opened her
mouth to say something . . . and then closed it again.

Things were not going too smoothly. If she was keeping her mouth shut, it meant they'd had a fight. If she was keeping her mouth shut, it meant that my brother had raised his voice.

Which is a rare thing.

My brother never gets annoyed, never says anything bad about anybody, doesn't have an unkind bone in his body, and does not judge his fellow man. My brother is from another planet. Venus, maybe . . .

We adore him. We ask him: "How do you manage to stay so calm?" He shrugs his shoulders: "I don't know." We ask him again: "Don't you ever feel like letting go sometimes? Saying really mean, nasty things?"

"But that's why I have you, gorgeous . . . " he replies, with an angelic smile.

Yes, we adore him. In fact, everybody adores him. Our nannies, his teachers, his professors, his colleagues at work, his neighbors . . . everybody.

When we were younger, we'd sprawl on the carpet in his bedroom, listening to his records and drowning him with kisses while he did our homework, and we played at imagining our future. Our predictions for Simon: "You are too nice . . . some bitch will get her claws into you."

Bingo.

I had a pretty good idea why they'd been arguing. It was probably because of me. I could reproduce their conversation down to the last sigh.

Yesterday afternoon, I asked my brother if they could

give me a lift. "What a question . . . " he said, politely offended, on the phone. After that, the charming chick must have thrown her tantrum, because coming to pick me up means a major detour. My brother must have shrugged his shoulders, and she'd have laid it on even thicker: "But darling, from her place to the road for Limousin . . . The Place Clichy is not exactly a shortcut, as far as I know . . . "

He had to force himself to be firm, they went to bed angry, and she slept at Hotel Cold Shoulder.

She got up in a bad mood. While drinking her organic chicory, she started up again: "No, really, your lazy sister, she could have gotten up and come out here . . . Honestly, it's hardly her work that's wearing her out, or is it?"

He didn't react. He was studying the map.

She went to sulk in her Kaufman & Broad bathroom (I remember our first visit . . . With some sort of purple chiffon scarf around her neck, she was twirling around among her potted plants and commenting on her Petit Trianon, absolutely gurgling: "Here we have the kitchen . . . so functional. And now the dining room . . . utterly convivial. And as for the living room . . . so versatile. Here's Léo's bedroom . . . isn't it playful? Now this is the laundry room . . . just indispensable. And of course the bathroom . . . double, natch. And as for our bedroom . . . so luminous. Here's . . . " It was as if she wanted to sell it to us. Simon drove us back to the station and just as we were leaving, we said, "You've got a beautiful house . . . " "Yes, it's functional," he echoed, nodding his head. Neither Lola nor Vincent nor I uttered a single word on the way back. We were all kind of sad, each in our own corner; we were probably thinking the same thing, that we had lost our older brother, and that life would be a lot tougher without him . . .), and then, she must have looked at her watch at least ten times between their house and my boulevard, she must have groaned at every traffic light, and when finally she blew the horn—because I'm sure she's the one who blew the horn—I didn't hear them.

Oh woe, oh woe is me.

My dear Simon, I am so sorry to have put you through all that . . .

Next time, I'll make other arrangements, I promise you.

I'll do better. I'll go to bed early. I won't drink anymore. I won't play cards.

By next time, I'll have settled down, you know . . . of course I will. I'll find someone. A nice boy. A white guy. An only son. A guy who's got a driver's license and a Toyota that runs on colza.

I'll get me one who works at the post office, because his dad works at the post office, and who'll put in his twenty-nine hours a week without ever getting sick. A non-smoker. That's just what I put on my Meetic profile. You don't believe me? Well, you'll see. Why are you laughing, you dork?

That way I won't bug you anymore on Saturday morning to go to the country. I'll tell my little honeybunch from the post office: "Hey honeybunch! Will you drive me to my cousin's wedding with your beautiful GPS that even includes Corsica and Martinique and Tahiti?" and wham, all taken care of.

And why are you laughing like an idiot, now? Do you think I'm not clever enough to manage the way other people do? To find myself a nice guy with a yellow cardigan and a Euro Disney badge? A fiancé I can go and buy Celio boxer shorts for during my lunch break? Oh, yes . . . just thinking about it makes me go all wobbly . . . a decent sort. Serious. Simple. Batteries included, not to mention the savings-account booklet.

And he'd never worry about things. And he'd be only too glad to compare prices in the store with the ones in the catalogue and he'd say, "No two ways about it, darling, the difference between Ikea and Habitat, you're really just paying for service . . . "

And we'll enter the house through the basement so as not to get the entrance dirty. And we'll leave our shoes at the bottom of the steps not to get the stairway dirty. And we'll be friends with the neighbors who will be incredibly nice. And we'll have a built-in barbecue and that will be really awesome for the kids, because the housing estate will be super safe like my sister-in-law says and . . .

Oh, bliss.

It was too awful. I fell asleep.

I stumbled out onto the parking lot of a gas station somewhere on the outskirts of Orléans. Feeling groggy as hell. Woozy and drooly. I had trouble keeping my eyes open and my hair felt incredibly heavy. I even put my hand up to it, just to make sure it really was hair.

Simon was waiting by the cash register. Carine was powdering her nose.

I stationed myself by the coffee machine.

It took me at least thirty seconds to realize that my cup was ready. I drank it without sugar and without much conviction. I must have pressed the wrong button. There was a weird, faintly tomato-ish taste to my cappuccino.

Oh, man . . . It's going to be a long day.

We got back in the car without saying a word. Carine took a moist alcohol towelette from her make up bag to disinfect her hands.

Carine always disinfects her hands when she's been in public places.

For hygiene's sake.

Because Carine actually sees the germs.

She can see their furry little legs and their horrible mouths.

That's why she never takes the métro. She doesn't like trains, either. She can't help but think about the people who put their feet on the seats and stick their boogers under the armrest.

Her kids are not allowed to sit on a bench or to touch the railings. She has major issues about going to the playground. And issues about letting them use the slide. She has issues with the trays at McDonald's and she has *a ton* of issues about swapping Pokémon cards. She totally freaks out with butchers who don't wear gloves or little salesgirls who don't use tongs to serve her her croissant. She gets downright paralytic if the school organizes group picnics or outings to the swimming pool where all the kids have to hold hands as a prelude to passing on their fungal infections.

Life, for Carine, is exhausting.

Her business with the disinfectant towelettes really gets up my nose.

The way she always thinks other people must be sackfuls of germs. The way she always peers at their fingernails when she shakes hands. The way she never trusts anyone. Always hiding behind her scarf. Always telling her kids to be careful.

Don't touch. It's dirty.

Get your hands out of there.

Don't share.

Don't go out in the street.

Don't sit on the ground or I'll smack you!

Always washing their hands. Always washing their mouths. Always making sure they pee exactly ten centimeters above the bowl, dead center, and that they never ever let their lips touch someone's cheek when they go to kiss them. Always judging the other moms by the color of their kids' ears.

Always.

Always judging.

I don't like the sound of any of it. What's worse, when you go to dinner at her family's they have no compunction about mouthing off about Arabs.

Carine's dad calls them ragheads.

He says, "I pay taxes so those ragheads can have ten kids."

He says, "What I'd do with 'em, I'd stick 'em all in a boat and torpedo the whole lot of them, every last parasite, I would."

And he likes to say, "France is a country full of bums and people on welfare. A country full of losers."

And often, to finish, he goes like this: "I work the first six months of the year for my family and the next six for the state, so don't go talking to me about poor people and the unemployed, okay? I work one day out of two so Mamadou can go knock up his ten wives, so don't go lecturing me, okay?"

There was one lunch in particular. I don't like remembering it. It was for little Alice's baptism. We were all at Carine's parents' place near Le Mans.

Her father runs a Casino (the supermarket, not the Las Vegas variety), and that day, when I saw him down at the end of his little paved driveway between his artsy-fartsy wrought iron lamp and his gleaming Audi, I really understood the meaning of the word *complacent.* That mixture of stupidity and arrogance. His unshakeable self-satisfaction. That blue cashmere sweater stretched over his huge gut and that weird way—real friendly-like—he has of reaching out his hand to you even though he already hates you.

I'm ashamed when I think back on that lunch. I'm ashamed, and I'm not the only one. Lola and Vincent aren't too proud, either, I don't think . . .

Simon wasn't there when the conversation began to degenerate. He was out in the garden building a cabin for his son.

He must be used to it. He must know that it's better just to get out of there when fat Jacquot starts mouthing off . . .

Simon is like us: he doesn't like shouting matches at the end of a nice dinner, he hates conflict and runs like hell from power struggles. He says it's a waste of good energy and that you have to keep your strength for more worthwhile struggles in life. That with people like his father-in-law, you're fighting a losing battle.

And when you talk to him about the rise of the extreme right, he shakes his head: "Bah . . . they're just the dregs on the bottom of the lake. What can you do, it's only human. Best leave well enough alone, otherwise they'll rise to the surface."

How can he stand those family dinners? How can he even help his father-in-law trim the hedge?

He concentrates on Léo's cabins.

He concentrates on the moment he'll take his little boy

by the hand and they'll go off together into the deep and silent woods.

I'm ashamed because on that particular day, we didn't dare say a thing.

Once again we didn't dare say a thing. We didn't react to the words of that rabid shopkeeper who'll never see any farther than his distant navel.

We didn't contradict him, or leave the table. We went on slowly chewing every mouthful, thinking it was enough just to register what a jerk the guy was while pulling hard on all our loose threads, trying to wrap ourselves in what might remain of our dignity.

What wretches we were. Cowards, incredible cowards . . .

Why are we like that, all four of us? Why are we so intimidated by people who shout louder than others? Why do aggressive people make us go completely to pieces?

What is wrong with us? Where does a good upbringing end and spinelessness begin?

We've talked about it a lot. We beat our breasts over pizza crust and makeshift ashtrays. We don't need anyone to force us to. We're big enough to go about it ourselves, and no matter how many empty bottles we have at the end, we always come to the same conclusion. That if we are like this—silent and determined but absolutely useless when it comes to jerks like him—it is precisely because we haven't got a shred of self-confidence. We are sorely lacking in self-esteem.

We don't love our own selves.

We don't think we're all that important.

Not even important enough to splutter our indignation onto old man Molinoux's vest. Or to believe for one second that our squawking could ever influence his line of thought. Or to hope that a gesture of disgust like tossing our napkins onto the table or knocking over our chairs might have the slightest impact on the ways of the world.

What would that good taxpayer have thought if we had given him a piece of our mind and left his demesne with our heads held high? He would simply have battered his wife all evening with remarks like: "What complete pricks. Total pricks. I mean, have you ever seen such a hopeless bunch of pricks?"

And why should the poor woman be subjected to that?

Who are we to spoil the party for twenty people?

So you might say that it isn't cowardice. You might allow that it's actually wisdom. Acknowledge that we know when to stand back. That we don't like to stir shit up. That we're more honest than those people who protest all the time but never manage to change a thing.

Or at least that's what we figure, to make ourselves feel better. We remind each other that we're young and already far too lucid. And that we're head and shoulders above the ant farm, so stupidity can't really reach us up here. We don't really give a damn. We have other things, each other for a start. We are rich in other ways.

All we have to do is look inside.

We have a lot going on in our heads. Stuff that's light years from that man's racist ranting. There's music, and literature. There are places to stroll, hands to hold, refuges. Bits of shooting stars copied out onto credit card receipts,

pages torn out of books, happy memories and horrible
ones. Songs with refrains on the tips of our tongues. Mes-
sages we've kept, blockbusters we loved, gummy bears,
and scratched vinyl records. Our childhood, our solitude,
our first emotions, and our projects for the future. All the
hours we stayed up late, all the doors held open. Buster
Keaton's antics. Armand Robin's brave letter to the
Gestapo and Michel Leiris's battering ram of clouds. The
scene where Clint Eastwood turns around and says, "One
thing though . . . don't kid yourself, Francesca . . . " and
the one in *The Best of Youth* where Nicola Carati stands up
for his patients at the trial of their torturer. The dances on
Bastille Day in Villiers. The scent of quinces in the cellar.
Our grandparents, Monsieur Racine's saber, his gleaming
breastplate, our country kid illusions and the nights before
our finals. Our favorite comics: Mam'zelle Jeanne's rain-
coat when she climbs on behind Gaston on his motorbike,
or François Bourgeon's *Les Passagers du vent.* The opening
lines of the book by André Gorz dedicated to his wife,
which Lola read to me last night on the telephone when
we'd just spent ages bad-mouthing love, yet again: "You're
about to turn eighty-two. You've gotten six centimeters
shorter, you weigh only forty-five kilos, and you are still
beautiful, gracious, and desirable." Marcello Mastroianni
in *Dark Eyes*; gowns by Cristóbal Balenciaga. The way the
horses would smell of dust and dry bread when you got
off the school bus in the evening. The Lalannes, each
working in their own studio with a garden in between.
The night we repainted the rue des Vertus, and the time
we slipped a stinking herring skin under the terrace of the
restaurant where that stupid ass Poêle Tefal worked. And
the time we rode at the back of a truck, face down on sheets

of cardboard, and Vincent read us all of Orwell's *Road to Wigan Pier* out loud. Simon's face when he heard Björk for the first time, or Monteverdi, in the parking lot of the Macumba.

So much silliness and regret, and the soap bubbles at Lola's godfather's funeral . . .

Our lost loves, our torn letters, and our friends on the other end of the line. All those unforgettable nights, and how we were forever moving house, and all the strangers we bashed into all those times we had to run to catch a bus that might not wait . . .

All of that, and more.
Enough to keep our souls alive.
Enough to know not to try to talk back to stupid idiots.
Let them croak.
They'll anyway.
They'll die all alone while we're at the movies.

That's what we tell ourselves so we'll feel better about not getting up and leaving the table that day.

Then there's the obvious fact that all of it—our apparent indifference, our discretion, and our weakness, too—it's all our parents' fault.

It's their fault—or should I say it's thanks to them.

Because they're the ones who taught us about books and music. Who talked to us about other things and forced us to see things in a different light. To aim higher and farther. But they also forgot to give us confidence, because they thought that it would just come naturally.

That we had a special gift for life, and compliments might spoil our egos.

They got it wrong.

The confidence never came.

So here we are. Sublime losers. We just sit there in silence while the loudmouths get their way, and any brilliant response we might have come up with is nipped in the bud, and all we're left with is a vague desire to puke.

Maybe it was all the whipped cream we ate . . .

I remember how one day we were all together, the whole family, on a beach near Hossegor—because we rarely went anywhere together as a family—family with a capital F, that wasn't really our style—our Pop (our dad never wanted us to call him Dad and so when people were surprised we would say it was because of May 1968. That was a pretty good excuse, we thought, "May '68," like a secret code, it was as if we were saying "It's because he's from planet Zorg")—so our Pop, as I was saying, must have looked up and said, "Kids, you see this beach?"

(Any idea how huge the Côte d'Argent is?)

"Well, do you know what you are, you kids, on the scale of the universe?"

(Yeah! Kids who aren't allowed any doughnuts!)

"You are this grain of sand. Just this one, right here. And that's it."

We believed him.

Our loss.

"What's that smell?" said Carine.

I was spreading Madame Rashid's paste all over my legs.

"What . . . what on earth is that stuff?"

"I'm not sure exactly. I think it's honey or caramel mixed with wax and spices."

"Oh my God, that's horrible! That is disgusting! And you're going to do *that, here*?"

"Where else can I do it? I can't go to the wedding like this. I look like a yeti."

My sister-in-law turned away with a sigh.

"Be very careful of the seat. Simon, turn off the A/C so I can open the window."

Please, I muttered, my teeth clenched.

Madame Rashid had wrapped this huge lump of Turkish delight in a damp cloth. "Next time come see me, I take care of you next time. I do your little love garden. After you see, how he like it, your man, when I make it all gone, he go crazy with you and he give you anything you want . . . " she assured me with a wink.

I smiled. Just a faint smile. I'd just made a spot on the armrest and now I had to juggle with my Kleenex. What a mess.

"And are you going to get dressed in the car, too?"

"We'll stop somewhere just before . . . Hey, Simon? Can you find me a little side road somewhere?"

"One that smells of hazelnuts?"

"I should hope so!"

"And Lola?" asked Carine.

"What about Lola?"

"Is she coming?"

"I don't know."

"You don't know?" She looked startled.

"No. I don't know."

"This is unbelievable. Nobody ever knows anything with you guys. It's always the same thing. Complete bohemian shambles. Can't you just for once get your act together? Just a little bit?"

"I spoke to her on the phone yesterday," I said curtly. "She wasn't feeling too good and she didn't know yet whether she could make it."

"Well well, what a surprise."

Oooh, just listen to that condescending tone of hers . . .

"What's surprising about it?" I said, between my teeth.

"Oh, dear! Nothing. Nothing surprises me anymore with you lot. And if Lola is that way, it's her fault, too. It's what she wanted, right? She really has a gift for ending up in the most incredible fixes. You just don't go around—"

I could see Simon in the rearview mirror, a few lines suddenly creasing his brow.

"Well, as far as I'm concerned . . . "

Yes. Exactly. As far as you're concerned . . .

" . . . the problem with Lo—"

"Stop!" I exploded, in midair, "stop right there. I didn't get enough sleep, so . . . leave it for later."

Then she got all huffy: "Oh, well! No one can ever say a thing in this family. The least little comment and there's a knife at your throat, it's ridiculous."

Simon was trying to catch my eye.

"And you think that's funny, huh? Both of you, you think it's funny, don't you? It's unbelievable. Completely childish. I'm entitled to my opinion, no? Since you won't listen and no one can say a thing to you, and no one ever does say a thing, you're untouchable. You never stop to question the status quo. Well, I'm going to give you a piece of my mind—"

But we don't want a piece of your mind, sweetheart.

"I think this protectionism of yours, this way you have of acting like 'we're all in this together and the rest of you can go hang' won't do you any favors. It's not the least bit constructive."

"But what *is* constructive here on earth, Carine love?"

"Oh please, spare me, not that, too. Don't start on your pseudo-Socrates disabused philosophers act. It's pathetic, at your age. And have you finished with that goop, it really is revolting—"

"Yeah, yeah . . . " I assured her, rolling the ball over my white calves, "I'm almost done."

"Aren't you going to use some sort of cream, after-wards? Your pores are in a state of shock now, you've got to re-moisturize your skin otherwise you'll be covered in little red spots until tomorrow."

"Darn, I forgot to bring anything."

"Don't you have your face cream?"

"No."

"Or moisturizer?"

"No."

"Night cream?"

"No."

"You didn't bring *anything?*"

She was horrified.

"I did. I brought a toothbrush, and some toothpaste, and *L'Heure Bleue*, and some condoms, and mascara, and a tube of pink Labello."

She was shattered.

"That is all you have in your toilet bag?"

"Uh . . . it's in my handbag. I don't have a toilet bag."

She sighed, and started foraging in her make up bag, and she handed me a big white tube.

"Here, put some of this on."

I thanked her with a genuine smile. She was pleased. She may be a first-class pain but she does like to please others. Credit where credit is due.

And she really doesn't like to leave pores in a state of shock. It breaks her heart.

After a few minutes she added, "Garance?"

"Mm-hmm?"

"You know what I think is deeply unfair?"

"The profit that Seph—"

"Well, that you'll be lovely no matter what. Just a little bit of lip gloss and a touch of mascara, and you'll be beautiful. It hurts me to say it, but it's true . . . "

I was floored. It was the first time in years she'd said something nice to me. I could have kissed her, but then right away she calmed me down:

"Hey, don't use up the whole tube! It's not L'Oréal, I'll have you know."

That's Carine all over. No sooner does she suspect you might catch her red-handed in a moment of weakness than, systematically, after the caress, she plants the needle.

Pity. She's missing out on a lot of good moments. It

would have been a good moment for her if I'd wrapped myself around her neck without warning. A big bare kiss, between two trucks . . . Nope. She always has to spoil everything.

I often think I ought to take her to my place as an intern for a day or two to give her a few lessons in life.

So that she could let her guard down for once, let herself go, roll up her sleeves, and forget about other people's miasma.

It makes me sad to see her like that, straitjacketed by all her prejudices and incapable of tenderness. And then I remember that she was raised by the dashing Jacques and Francine Molinoux at the far end of a dead-end street in the residential outskirts of Le Mans and I figure that, all things considered, she isn't doing so badly after all . . .

The cease-fire didn't last, and Simon was used for target practice.

"You're driving too fast. Lock the doors, we're getting near the tollbooth. What on earth is that on the radio? I didn't mean twenty miles an hour though, did I? Why'd you turn the A/C off? Watch out for those bikers. Are you sure you've got the right map? Can't you read the road signs, *please?* It's so stupid, I'm sure the gas cost less back there . . . Be careful in the curves, can't you see I'm painting my nails? Hey . . . are you doing it on purpose, or what?"

I can just make out the back of my brother's neck in the hollow space of his headrest. That fine, straight neck, his hair cut short.

I wonder how he can stand it, I wonder if he ever

dreams of tying her to a tree and running off as fast as his legs can carry him.

Why does she speak to him like that? Does she even know who she's talking to? Does she even know that the man sitting next to her was the god of scale models? The ace of Meccano sets? A Lego System genius?

A patient little boy who could spend several months building an awesome planet, with dried lichen for the ground and hideous creatures made of bread rolled in spiders' webs?

A stubborn little tyke who entered every contest and won nearly all of them: Nesquik, Ovomaltine, Babybel, Caran d'Ache, Kellogg's, and the Mickey Mouse Club?

One year, his sand castle was so beautiful that the members of the jury disqualified him: they claimed he'd had help. He cried all afternoon and our granddad had to take him to the crêperie to console him. He drank three whole mugs of hard cider, one after the other.

First time he ever got roaring drunk.

Does she even know that for months her good little lapdog of a hubby wore a satin Superman cape day and night that he folded up conscientiously in his schoolbag whenever it was time to go through the gate into the schoolyard? He was the only boy who knew how to repair the photocopy machine in the town hall. And he was the only one who'd ever seen Mylène Carois's underpants—she was the butcher's daughter, Carois & Fils. (He hadn't dared to tell her that he was not all that interested.)

Simon Lariot, a discreet man, who'd always made his own sweet way, gracefully, without bothering a soul.

*

Who never threw tantrums, or whined, or asked for a thing. Who went through prep school and got into engineering school without ever grinding his teeth or resorting to Tenormin. Who didn't want to make a big deal when he did well, and blushed to the tips of his ears when the headmistress of the Lycée Stendhal kissed him in the street to congratulate him.

The same big boy who can laugh like an idiot for exactly twenty minutes when he's smoking a joint and who knows *every single* trajectory of *every single* spaceship in *Star Wars*.

I'm not saying he's a saint, I'm saying he's better than one.

Why, then? Why does he let people walk all over him? It's a mystery to me. I've lost track of the number of times I've wanted to shake him, to open his eyes and get him to pound his fist on the table. Countless times.

One day Lola tried. He sent her packing and barked that it was his life, after all.

Which is true. It's his life. But we're the ones who are saddened by it.

Which is idiotic, in a way. We've got more than enough to keep us busy on our own turf.

He opens up the most with Vincent. Because of the Internet. They write each other all the time, send each other corny jokes and links for websites where they can find old vinyl LPs and used guitars and other model enthusiasts. Simon made himself a great friend in Massachusetts, they swap photos of their respective remote-controlled boats. The guy's name is Cecil (Simon can't pronounce it right, he says, See-sull) W. Thurlington, and he lives in a big house on Martha's Vineyard.

Lola and I think it sounds really . . . chic. Martha's Vineyard . . . "The cradle of the Kennedys," as they say in *Paris Match.*

We have this fantasy where we take the plane and then go up to Cecil's private beach and we shout, "Yoo-hoo! Darling See-sull! We are Simon's sisters! We are so very ahn-shahn-tay!"

We picture him wearing a navy blue blazer, with an old rose cotton sweater thrown over his shoulders, and off-white linen slacks. Straight out of a Ralph Lauren ad.

When we threaten to dishonor Simon with our plan, he tends to lose some of his cool.

"Hey, are you doing it on purpose or what?"

"Well how many coats do you have to put on, anyway?" he says eventually.

"Three."

"Three coats?"

"Base, color, and fixer."

"Oh . . ."

"Be careful, and at least warn me when you're about to brake."

He raises his eyebrows. No. Correction. One eyebrow.

What can he be thinking when he raises his right eyebrow like that?

We ate rubbery sandwiches at one of those freeway rest stops. It was revolting. I'd been plugging for a *plat du jour* at one of the truck stops but "they don't know how to wash the lettuce." True. I'd forgotten. So, three vacuum wrapped sandwiches, please. (Infinitely more hygienic.)

"It may not be good, but at least we know what we're eating!"

That's one way of looking at it.

We were sitting outside next to the garbage dumpsters. You could hear "brrrrammm" and "brrrroommm" every two seconds but I wanted to smoke a cigarette and Carine cannot stand the smell of tobacco.

"I have to use the restroom," she announced, with a pained expression. "I don't suppose it's too luxurious . . . "

"Why don't you go in the grass?" I asked.

"In front of everyone? Are you crazy?"

"Just go a little bit further, that way. I'll come with you if you want."

"No."

"Why not?"

"I'll get my shoes dirty."

"I don't think so, the time it will take you . . . "

She got up without condescending to answer.

"You know, Carine," I said solemnly, "the day you learn to enjoy having a wee in the grass, you'll be a much happier person."

She took her towelettes.

"Everything is just fine, thank you."

I turned to my brother. He was staring at the cornfield as if he were trying to count every single ear. He didn't look too great.

"You okay?"

"I'm okay," he replied, without turning around.
"Doesn't look it."
He was rubbing his face.
"I'm tired."
"What of?"
"Of everything."
"You? I don't believe you."
"And yet it's true."
"Is it your work?"
"My work. My life. Everything."
"Why are you telling me this?"
"Why wouldn't I tell you?"

He had his back to me again.
"Yo, Simon! Hey, what's going on? Don't talk like this. You're the hero of the family, in case you need reminding."
"Well, yeah, that's kind of the problem . . . the hero is tired."

I was speechless. This was the first time I'd ever seen him in such a state.
If Simon was beginning to have his doubts, where were we headed?

Just then—and to me this was a miracle, although on the other hand it doesn't surprise me, and I kiss the patron saint of brothers and sisters who has been watching over us now for nearly thirty-five years, and who has never been out of work, poor guy—his cell rang.
It was Lola, who had finally made up her mind, and was asking him if he could stop and pick her up at the station in Châteauroux.

*

Our spirits immediately revived. Simon put his cell back in his pocket and asked me for a cigarette. Carine came back, scrubbing her arms right up to her elbows. She immediately reminded her husband of the precise number of cancer victims who had died because of . . . He gave a limp wave of his hand as if he were chasing a fly and she walked away, coughing.

Lola was coming. Lola would be with us. Lola hadn't let us down, and the rest of the world could just go hang.
Simon put on his dark glasses.
He was smiling.
His little Lola was on the train . . .

They have this special thing between them. First of all, they're closest in age, only eighteen months apart, and they were really *children* together.
They were the ones who were always getting up to mischief. Lola had an irrepressible imagination and Simon was pliant (already . . .). They ran away. They got lost. They got into fights, tormented each other, made up. Mom likes to tell us how Lola would needle him all the time, always going into his bedroom to bug him, grabbing the book from his hands or kicking something straight into his Playmobil. My sister doesn't like to recall these acts of war (she worries she's being lumped in the same basket with Carine), so then our mom senses that she'd better change tack and she adds that Lola was always eager for something new, she'd invite all the kids in the neighborhood and invent all kinds of new games. She was like one of those cool scout leaders who can come up with a thousand ideas a minute, and she watched

over her big brother like a broody hen. She'd make all sorts of inedible snacks for him with mustard and Nutella and she'd come and lift him out of his Legos when Grendizer or Captain Harlock was on television.

Lola and Simon grew up during the Golden Age. When there was Villiers. When we all lived out in the sticks and our parents were happy together. For them the world began outside the front door and ended on the far side of the village.

They would streak across fields pursued by imaginary bulls, and creep into abandoned houses haunted by ghosts that weren't imaginary at all.

They rang the bell at old mother Margeval's until she was ripe for the asylum; they destroyed the hunters' traps; they pissed into washtubs, nicked the teacher's dirty magazines, stole firecrackers, set off the ones called mammoth, and rescued little kittens that some bastard had sealed up alive in a plastic bag.

Boom. Seven kittens all at once. You bet Pop was happy!

And the day the Tour de France came through *our* village . . . Lola and Simon went and bought fifty baguettes and sold sandwiches by the dozen. With their earnings they bought practical jokes and gags, and sixty Malabar candies, and a jump-rope for me, and a little trumpet for Vincent (already!), and the latest *Yoko Tsuno*.

Yes, childhood was different back then . . . They knew what an oarlock was, and they smoked creepers and knew the taste of gooseberries. And then there came the biggest major significant event of all, what a huge impact it had, and it happened right behind the door to the shed:

Today ~~Ar~~ April 8 we saw the preist waring shorts.

*

Then they went through our parents' divorce, together. Vincent and I were still too little. We only really figured out what a raw deal we were getting when the day came to move house. But they'd been able to witness the entire show. They would get up in the middle of the night and go and sit side by side at the top of the stairs to listen to the "discussion." One night Pop knocked over the humungous kitchen cupboard and Mom drove off in the car.

While ten steps up from there they sat sucking their thumbs.

It's stupid to go on telling that side of the story: they were close for any number of reasons that, in the long run, meant more than the tough times. But still . . .

For Vincent and me it was completely different. We were city brats. Less bicycling and more time in front of the box. We had no idea how to stick on a rubber repair patch but we did know how to dodge a subway fare or repair a skateboard or sneak into the movies through the emergency exit.

And then Lola got sent to boarding school, and there was no one around anymore to fill our heads with whispered mischief or chase after us in the garden . . .

We wrote to each other every week. She was my beloved older sister. I idealized her; I sent her drawings and wrote poems to her. When she came home she would ask me whether Vincent had behaved himself during her absence. Of course not, I'd say, of course not. And I'd describe in detail all the horrible things I'd had to undergo the previous week. At which point, to my supreme satisfaction, she'd drag him into the bathroom to acquaint him with the riding crop.

The louder my brother screamed, the wider I grinned.

And then one day, to make it even better, I wanted to see him suffer. To my complete, flabbergasted horror, I burst in to find my sister whipping a bolster, while Vincent bleated in time, reading his *Boule et Bill* comic book. A mega disappointment. On that day, Lola fell from her pedestal.

Which turned out to be a good thing. Now we were the same height.

Nowadays she's my best friend. We're sort of like Montaigne and La Boétie, for example . . . Because she is who she is, and I am who I am. The fact that this young woman of thirty-two years of age is also my older sister is totally beside the point. Well, maybe not totally, it's just fortunate we didn't have to waste time trying to find each other.

She's all into Montaigne's *Essays*—she likes grand theories, the notion that one is punished for stubbornly wanting, and philosophy is just learning how to die. Give me the *Discourse of Voluntary Servitude*—infinite abuse and all those tyrants who are great because we are on our knees. She'll take true knowledge, I'll take tribunals. As the wise man himself said: "I was so grown and accustomed to be always her double in all places and in all things, that methinks I am no more than half of myself."

And yet we are very different . . . She is afraid of her own shadow; I sit on mine. She copies out sonnets, I download samples. She admires painters, I prefer photographers. She never tells you what is in her heart, I speak my mind. She avoids conflict, I like things to be perfectly clear. She likes to be "a little bit tipsy," I prefer to drink. She doesn't like going out, I don't like going home. She doesn't know how to have fun, I don't know when it's time to get some sleep. She hates gambling, I hate losing. Her embrace is all-encompassing, my kindness has its limits. She never gets annoyed, I'm forever blowing a gasket.

She says the world belongs to early risers, I beg her to tone it down. She's romantic, I'm pragmatic. She got married, I flitter and flirt. She can't sleep with a guy unless she's in love, I can't sleep with a guy unless there's a condom. She needs me.

Ditto.

She doesn't judge, she takes me as I am. With my gray complexion and my black thoughts. Or my rosebud complexion and my buttercup thoughts. Lola knows how it feels to lust after a pea jacket or a pair of heels. She completely understands how much fun it can be to max out a credit card then feel guilty as hell when the bill comes. Lola spoils me. She holds the curtain for me when I'm in the fitting room, and she always tells me I'm beautiful and no, not at all, it doesn't make my butt look big. She asks, every time, how my love life is going, and pulls a face when I tell her about my lovers.

Whenever we haven't seen each other in a long while she takes me to a brasserie, Bofinger or Balzar, to look at the guys. I focus on the ones at nearby tables; she zeroes in on the waiters. She is fascinated by those dorky dudes in tight waistcoats. She can't take her eyes off them, she imagines life stories for them straight out of a Claude Sautet film, and she dissects their perfectly trained mannerisms. The funny thing is that at some point you always see one of them going out the door at the end of his shift. And then she wonders what she ever saw in him. Jeans or even jogging pants in lieu of the long white apron, and an offhand shout to a co-worker as he takes his leave: "Bye, Bernard!"

"Bye, Mimi. You here tomorrow?"

"No way. Dream on, dude."

Lola looks down and traces patterns in the sauce on her plate with her fingertips. Another one gone . . .

We sort of lost sight of each other for a while. First boarding school, then studies, then her wedding, vacations at her in-laws', dinner parties . . .

We still knew how to hug, but we'd lost the art of letting ourselves go. She had changed sides. Teams, rather. She wasn't playing *against* us so much as playing for a league that was, well, kind of boring. Some sort of half-assed *cricket,* for example, with lots of incomprehensible rules, where you go running after something you never see, and it can really hurt, too . . . some sort of leathery thing with a cork core. (Hey, Lola! I didn't mean to, but I've just summed it all up!)

Whereas we younger kids were still busy with a lot more basic things. A lovely lawn⇒yabba dabba doo! Heineken and neckin'. Tall boys wearing white polo shirts⇒honk, honk! The bat in your behind. Well, you see what I'm driving at . . . Not really mature enough yet for strolls around the Bassin de Neptune at Versailles . . .

There you have it. We'd wave to each other from a distance. She made me the godmother of her first child and I made her the trustee of my first broken heart (and did I weep, a regular baptismal fount), but between two of these sort of major events there was not much going on. Birthdays, family luncheons, a few cigarettes shared on the sly so her honey wouldn't see, a knowing look, or her head on my shoulder when we'd browse through old photos . . .

That was life. Her life, at any rate.

Respect.

And then she came back to us. Covered in ash, with the lunatic gaze of the pyromaniac who's just handed in his box of matches. Plaintiff in a divorce that no one expected. It has to be said she played her cards close to her chest, the vixen. Everyone thought she was happy. I think we even admired her for it, for the way she'd found the exit so easily and quickly. "Lola's got it all sorted out," we'd say, without bitterness or envy. Lola is still champ when it comes to treasure hunts . . .

And then crash bang boom. A change of program.

She just showed up at my place one day, and at a time that wasn't like her at all. At bath and bedtime story time. She was in tears, apologizing. She truly believed that it was the people around her who justified her existence on this earth, and everything else—her secret life and all the little nooks and crannies of her soul—was not really all that important. What was important was being cheerful and carrying your yoke as if it were the easiest thing in the world. And when things got harder, there was always solitude, drawing, and going for ever longer walks behind the baby carriage, and the kids' books and family life that offered such a deep and comfortable refuge.

So it seemed. That little red hen in the Père Castor series, she was right, the perfect model of housewifely escapism . . .

Red Hen's the perfect housewife:
Not a speck of dust on the furniture,
The flowers all in their vases,
And carefully ironed curtains at every window.
What a treat to see her house!

Except that, here's the thing, Lola had gone out and cut that little red hen's throat.

I was stunned, like everyone else. I didn't know what to say. She'd never complained, never let on that she had her doubts, and she'd just given birth to another adorable little boy. She was loved. She had it all, as they say. "They" being a load of idiots.

How are you supposed to react when you find out your whole solar system is off its orbit? What are you supposed to say? For Christ's sake—she was the one who'd always shown *us* the way. We trusted her. Or at least I trusted her. We sat on the floor for what seemed like ages, knocking back the vodka. She was in tears, and over and over she said she didn't know where the hell she was going, then she'd fall silent and burst into tears again. No matter what she decided, she'd be miserable. She could stay, or she could go: life was no longer worth living.

Bison grass to the rescue. Together, we managed to shake her out of her apathy. Hey! She wasn't the only one who'd been shipwrecked. When the instruction booklet is as fat as a Manhattan phone book and you're running circles on a lawn the size of a pocket handkerchief with no one at your side, or at least not your lawful wedded, well, at the end of the day . . . time to hit the road, girl!

She wasn't listening.

"And what about the kids . . . couldn't you hang on a bit longer, for their sake?" I eventually murmured, handing her another pack of Kleenex. My question dried her tears on the spot. I really didn't get it, did I? It was for their sake, this whole mess. To spare them the suffering. So that they'd never hear their parents fighting and crying in the middle of the night. Besides, you can't grow up in a house where people don't love each other anymore—or can you?

No. You can't. You can grow, maybe, but not grow up.

What came after that was more sordid. Lawyers, tears, blackmail, sorrow, sleepless nights, fatigue, self-sacrifice, guilt, it hurts me more than it hurts you, aggression, recrimination, courthouse, taking sides, appeal, lack of air, heads leaning against the wall. And in the midst of it all, two little boys with clear bright eyes for whose sake she went on playing the clown, telling them her bedside stories about farting princes and airhead princesses. This is all fairly recent, and the embers are still warm. It wouldn't take much for the sorrow she felt at the sorrow she caused to drown her again, and I know there are mornings she has trouble getting out of bed. She confessed the other day that when the kids went off with their dad she stood for ages watching herself crying in the mirror in the hall.

As if she were trying to dilute herself.

That was why she didn't want to come to this wedding. To have to deal with family. All the uncles and aging aunts and distant cousins. All these people who didn't get divorced. Who settled. Who found other ways. Who'll look at her with their vaguely sympathetic expressions—or maybe they're just dismayed. Then all the theatrics: the virginal white dress, the Bach cantatas, the vows of eternal fidelity you learned by heart, and the schoolboy speeches, the two hands joined on the knife of the wedding cake, and Strauss waltzes by the time your feet are really beginning to ache. But more than anything else: the kids. Other people's kids.

The ones who'll be running all over the place all day long, with their ears red from sipping the dregs in people's glasses, with stains on their best clothes, begging not to have to go to bed yet.

Kids are the whole point of family reunions—and they console us for having to attend them.

They're always the nicest things to look at. They're always the first ones on the dance floor, and the only ones who will dare to tell you that the cake is disgusting. They fall madly in love for the first time in their lives and fall asleep exhausted on their mommies' laps. Pierre was supposed to be the page boy, and he'd worked out that his cybersaber would fit perfectly beneath his cummerbund; he wondered, too, whether he'd be able to filch a few coins from the collection basket. But Lola had confused the dates on the judge's calendar: it wasn't her weekend for the kids. So no little baskets, no rice battles outside the church. We had suggested she call Thierry to see if she couldn't swap weekends with him: she didn't even reply.

But now she was coming! And Vincent would be waiting for us! We'd be able to sit down at a table off to one side behind a tent, just the four of us and a few bottles we'd grab on the way, and we could indulge our comments on Aunt Solange's hat, or the bride's hips, or how ridiculous our cousin Hubert looked with his hired top hat jammed down over his big sticking-out ears. (His mother would never entertain the possibility of having his ears pinned back, because "one must not undo the work of God.") (Wow. Lovely as the day is long, no?)

We would be reunited, the four of us, life picking us up where we'd left off.

Trumpets, sound! Larks, sing! It was time for some sibling swashbuckling—all for one and one for . . . and all that jazz.

W hy did you take this exit?"
"We're going to pick up Lola," said Simon.
"Where?" said his lady, in a strangled voice.
"At the station in Châteauroux."
"You're joking, right?"
"No, not at all. She'll be there in forty minutes."
"And why didn't you tell me?"
"I forgot. She only just called."
"When?"
"When we were at the freeway rest stop."
"I didn't hear the phone."
"You were in the restroom."
"I see . . . "
"What do you see?"
"Nothing."
Her lips said just the opposite.

"Is there a problem?" asked my brother.
"No. No problem. None at all. It's just that next time you should put a taxi sign on the roof of the car, it would make things clearer."
He didn't react. His knuckles went white.
Carine had left Léo and Alice with her mother so that, quote, *We can have a romantic weekend,* ellipsis, close quote.

But it looked like it might well be a hot, hot, hot one.

"And the rest of you . . . do you intend to sleep in the same hotel room as us, too?"

"No, no," I said, shaking my head, "don't worry."

"Did you book a room?"

"Well . . . no."

"Of course not. I suspected as much, to be honest."

"But it's not a problem! We'll sleep anywhere! We can go to Aunt Paule's!"

"Aunt Paule is full up. She told me as much already on the phone the day before yesterday."

"Well we just won't sleep and that's it!"

She muttered *godyerrude*, fiddling with the fringe on her pashmina.

I didn't understand.

Worse luck, the train was ten minutes late and when finally all the passengers had disembarked there was no sign of Lola.

Simon and I squeezed our butts.

"Are you sure you didn't confuse Châteauroux and Châteaudun?" squawked the shrew.

And then—yes, look . . . There she was . . . All the way at the end of the platform. She was in the last carriage, she must have boarded the train at the last minute, but there she was, walking toward us, waving her arms.

True to form and just the way I'd hoped to find her. A smile on her face, swinging her hips, wearing ballet flats, a white shirt, and a pair of old jeans.

*

And an amazing hat. With a huge brim and a wide black grosgrain ribbon.

She hugged me. "You look lovely," she said, "did you cut your hair?" She hugged Simon and stroked his back then she took off her hat so she wouldn't muss Carine's curls.

She'd had to travel in the bicycle carriage because she couldn't find a place to put her sombrero and now she asked us if we could make a detour by the station buffet so she could buy a sandwich. Carine looked at her watch and I took the time to grab a trash celeb magazine.

The gutter press. All that pretentious posturing . . .

We climbed back into the car, and Lola asked her sister-in-law if she would be willing to hold her hat on her lap. Oh, no problem, said she, with a somewhat forced smile. No problem.

My sister raised her chin as if to ask, What's going on? And I rolled my eyes skyward to reply, same old.

She smiled and asked Simon to put on some music.

Carine replied that she had a headache.

I smiled, too.

Then Lola asked whether someone had some nail polish for her toes. She asked again: no answer. Finally our favorite pharmacist handed her a little red bottle: "Mind the seat, okay?"

Then we swapped sister stories. I'll skip that scene. We have too many codes, shortcuts and grunts. Besides, without the soundtrack, it's meaningless.

All you sisters out there will know what I mean.

We were out in the boonies, Carine was reading the map and Simon was being raked over the coals. At some point he said, "Give that fucking map to Garance, she's the only one who has any sense of direction in this damned family!"

In the back, we looked at each other and frowned. Two swear words in the same sentence, with an exclamation mark to close . . . Things weren't going too well.

Shortly before we arrived at Aunt Paule's castle, Simon came upon a little lane with blackberry bushes on either side. It reminded us of the arbors in Villiers; we rushed over to the bushes and our voices were trembling. Carine didn't shift her butt from the car and called out to remind us that foxes piss on blackberry bushes.

We didn't take any notice.

Our mistake . . .

"Naturally. You've never heard of echinococcosis. The larvae of parasites are transmitted by urine, and—"

Mea culpa, mea maxima culpa, I lost it there for a minute: "That's all bullshit, big time! Foxes can piss wherever they like, they have the entire great outdoors! Every path and hedge and tree, wherever you look, why in hell would they come and piss *right here*? Right on *our* black-berries? What the hell are you saying? It drives me crazy, in the end . . . *That's* what makes me sick, people like you who always have to go spoiling everything . . . "

Sorry. Mea culpa. My fault. My very great fault. And I had promised myself I would behave. I had promised myself I'd stay calm and infinitely zen. This very morning, when I was looking at myself in the mirror, I wagged my finger at my reflection: Garance, don't go getting pissed off with Carine, okay? No drama-queen routine for once. But there, I blew it. I'm sorry. My humble apologies, etc. She spoiled our blackberries and the little bit of childhood that remained along with it. She presses all my buttons, I cannot stand her. One more remark and I'd make her eat Lola's sombrero.

She must have felt the back draft from the cannonball because she closed the car door and switched on the ignition. For the A/C.

That gets up my nose, too, that sort of thing, people who keep the engine on when they stop somewhere just so that they can keep their feet warm or their head cool. But anyway, never mind. We'll talk about global warming some other day. She'd locked herself in, which was something. Let's stay positive.

Simon stretched his legs while we got changed. I'd bought a magnificent sari in the Passage Brady right next to my house. It was turquoise, embroidered with gold thread and pearls and tiny bells. I had a little bodice with sleeves, a very tight straight long skirt slit high on the thigh, and a sort of huge cloth to wrap it all up in.

It was gorgeous.

Dangly earrings, all the amulets from Rajasthan around my neck, ten bangles on my right wrist and nearly twice that on my left.

"You look great," said Lola. "Incredible. Only you could get away with something like that. You've got such a lovely belly, all flat and muscular . . . "

"Hey," I said, feeling radiant but keeping a lid on it all the same, "six floors without an elevator . . . "

"Having kids has put my belly button between parentheses . . . You'll be careful, won't you? You'll use cream every day, and—"

I shrugged. My little spyglass couldn't see that far.

"Can you button me up?" she chirped, turning her back to me.

Lola was wearing her black faille dress for the umpteenth time. Very sober, sleeveless, with a round neckline and a million tiny cassock buttons all the way down the back.

"You haven't gone to too much expense for dear Hubert's wedding," I said.

She turned around with a smile.

"Hey . . . "

"What?"

"How much do you think I paid for the hat?"

"Two hundred?"

She shrugged.

"How much?"

"I can't tell you," she laughed, "it's too awful."

"Stop laughing, stupid, I can't do the buttons . . . "

Ballet flats were in that year. Hers were soft, with a little bow; mine were covered in golden sequins.

Simon clapped his hands. "C'mon, Bluebell Girls . . . All aboard!"

Holding tight to my sister's arm so I wouldn't stumble, I muttered, "I warn you, if that codfish asks me whether I'm going to a costume ball, I'll make her eat your hat."

*

Carine didn't get a chance to say a thing because I immediately had to get up again the minute I sat down. My skirt was too tight and I had to take it off if I didn't want to split it.

Sitting in my thong on those alpaca viscose car seats, I was . . . priestly.

We put on makeup using my compact while our resident echinococcosian double-checked the position of her clip-on earrings in the mirror on the sun visor.

Simon begged the three of us not to put on perfume at the same time.

We arrived in Podunk-on-Indre in good time. Behind the car I slipped on my skirt and we went to stand outside the entrance to the church while the good Podunkians looked on in astonishment from their windows.

The pretty young woman in gray and pink chatting with Uncle Georges over there was our mom. We rushed over to hug her, careful not to let her smudge us with lipstick.

She very diplomatically kissed her daughter-in-law first, complimenting her on her outfit, and then she turned to us with a laugh.

"Garance . . . You look superb . . . All that's missing is the bindi on your forehead!"

"That would take the cake," blurted Carine, before rushing over to our poor withered uncle. "Last I heard, this is not supposed to be a carnival . . . "

Lola made as if to hand me her hat, and we burst out laughing.

Our mother turned to Simon. "Were they this unbearable the entire trip?"

"Worse, even," he said gravely.

And added: "Where's Vincent? He's not with you?"

"No. He's at work."

"What do you mean, at work?"

"Well, back at his château . . . "

Our elder brother shrunk four inches in one go.

"But . . . I thought . . . He told me he was coming."

"I tried to persuade him but nothing doing. You know, Vincent and petits fours . . . "

Simon seemed devastated.

"I had a present for him. A really rare vinyl LP. Plus I really wanted to see him. I haven't seen him since Christmas. God, I'm so disappointed. I think I need a drink . . . "

Lola made a face.

"Caramba. Simon he no look very happy."

"I'll say," I muttered, glaring at Miss Spoilsport who was in the process of sucking up to all our aged aunties. "I'll say."

"Well, girls," said our mom, "you are splendid at any rate! You'll cheer him up, won't you, get your brother to dance some this evening, okay?"

And she moved away to pay the customary compliments here and there.

We followed her with our gaze—such a tiny little woman. Graceful, charming, full of energy, elegant, so much class . . .

A typical Parisienne.

Lola's face clouded over. Two adorable, laughing little girls were running to join the procession.

"Right," she said, "I think I'll go over and join Simon."

*

I stood there like a dork in the middle of the square; the folds of my sari suddenly felt all limp.

But not for long, in fact, because our cousin Sixtine came up to me with a cackle.

"Hey, Garance! Hare Krishna! You going to a costume ball or something?"

I smiled as best I could, and refrained from commenting on her poorly bleached mustache or her apple green suit from the Christine Laure chain in Besançon.

No sooner had she moved on than it was my Aunt Geneviève who renewed the attack: "Good Lord, is that you, my little Clémence? Good God, what's that metal thing in your bellybutton? It doesn't hurt now, does it?"

Okay, I thought, I'd better go and join Simon and Lola at the café . . .

They were both out on the terrace—their beers within reach, their heads thrown back to the sun, their legs stretched out before them.

I sat down to the sound of "cccrrrr" and ordered the same thing.

Elated, at peace at last, our lips festooned with foam, we observed the good folk standing in their doorways observing the good folk outside the church. A feast for the eyes.

"Hey, is that Olivier's new wife—after the first one cheated on him?"

"You mean the short brunette?"

"Nah, the blonde next to the Larochaufées . . . "

"Help. God, she's even uglier than the first one. Get a load of that handbag."

"A fake Gucci."

"Exactly. Even worse than the ones those street vendors in Italy sell. Fake Goo Chee from Beijing . . . "

"Disgraceful."

We could have gone on like that forever if Carine hadn't come looking for us.

"Are you coming? It's about to start."

"We're coming, we're coming . . . " said Simon, "let me finish my beer."

"But if we don't go right away," she insisted, "we'll have lousy seats and I won't see a thing."

"Go ahead, I said. I'll catch up with you."

"Hurry, okay?"

She was already sixty feet from us when she turned around to shout, "Stop in at that little grocery store on the other side of the square and buy some rice, okay?"

And she turned around yet again.

"Not the expensive kind, okay? Just some Uncle Ben's, like last time! For all we use it for . . . "

"Yeah, yeah . . . " he muttered, in his beard.

We saw the bride off in the distance on her daddy's arm. A girl who, soon enough, would have a whole string of little ones with big Mickey Mouse ears. We started counting how many people were arriving late, and cheered a choirboy who was streaking breathlessly across the square, tripping on his robe.

When the bells had fallen silent and the locals had returned to their oilcloth-covered tables, Simon said, "I'd like to see Vincent."

"You know, even if we call him now," said Lola, picking up her bag, "by the time he gets here . . . "

Just then a kid from the wedding party in flannel trousers and his hair parted on the side ran by. Simon called out to him.

"Hey kid, you want to win five rounds on the pinball machine?"

"Yeah!"

"Then go back and sit through mass and come and get us at the end of the sermon."

"Will you give me the money right now?"

Can you believe it. These kids nowadays are just too much.

"Here you go, you little crook. And no cheating, okay? Come and get us?"

"Do I have time for a round first?"

"Yeah, go on," sighed Simon, "but then after that head straight for the organ."

"Okay."

We sat on for a moment and then Simon said, "What if we go and see him?"

"Who?"

"Vincent, of course."

"But when?" I asked.

"Now."

"Now?"

"You mean: now?" echoed Lola.

"Are you off your head? You want to take the car and go there *now?*"

"My dear Garance, I think you have just perfectly summed up what I mean to say."

"Are you crazy?" said Lola. "We can't just get up and leave like that."

"Why not?" (He was hunting around for change in his pocket.) "Right. Are you girls coming?"

We didn't react. He raised his arms to the sky: "We're out of here, I said! Let's go! Time to cut and run, make a break. Take French leave, as they say."

"And what about Carine?"

He lowered his arms.

He took a pen out of his jacket and turned the beer coaster over.

We have gone to visit Vincent's château. I leave Carine with you. Her things are in front of your car. Hugs.

"Hey, kid! There's been a change of program. You don't need to go back to mass, just give this to the lady in gray with a pink hat, her name is Maud. Got it?"

The kid nodded.

"How you doing?"

"Two extra balls."

"Repeat what I just said to you."

"I write my name up on the honor roll and after that I give your beer coaster to a lady with a pink hat called Maud."

"Keep an eye out, and give it to her when she leaves the church."

"Okay, but it'll cost you more . . . "

He chuckled to himself.

Y ou forgot to leave the vanity case."
"Oops. Have to go back. She would never forgive
me."
I left it out in full view on top of her bag and then we
took off in a cloud of dust. As if we had just robbed a bank.

At first, no one dared say a thing. But there was this
nervous, happy excitement all the same, and Simon looked
in his rear view mirror every ten seconds.

Maybe we thought we'd hear the sirens of a police car
hot on our heels—compliments of Carine, rabid and foam-
ing at the mouth. But no, not a sound. Dead calm.

Lola was sitting in front and I leaned forward on my
elbows between the two of them. All waiting for someone
to break the awkward silence.

Simon switched on the radio; the Bee Gees were bleat-
ing, *And we're stayin' alive, stayin' alive. Ha ha ha ha . . .
stayin' alive, stayin' alive . . .*

Well what do you know. It was too good to be true. It
was a sign! The hand of God! (No. It was from Pattie to
Danny to celebrate the anniversary of the day they met at
the dance in Treignac in 1978, but we only found that out
afterwards.) We all started wailing in unison, "HA HA HA

HA! STAYIN' ALIIIIIII-VVVE!" while Simon zigzagged along the D114, yanking his tie off.

I put my jeans back on and Lola handed me her hat to put next to me on the seat.

Given what she'd paid for it, she was a bit disappointed.

"Hey . . . " I said, to try and console her, "you can wear it at my wedding . . . "

Peals of laughter resonating through the little car.

We'd rescued our good mood. We'd managed to eject the alien from our spacecraft.

All we needed now was to pick up the last crew member.

I hunted on the map for the hole where Vincent was living, and Lola played DJ. We could choose between France Bleu Creuse and Radio Gélinotte. Hardly the greatest sounds in the world but what did it matter? We were yakking away like crazy.

"I would never have dreamt you were capable of doing something like this," she said at last, turning to our chauffeur.

"As you get older you get wiser," he smiled, taking the cigarette I held out to him.

We'd been driving for two hours and I was telling them about my stay in Lisbon when I—

"What is it?" said Lola anxiously.

"Did you see that?"

"See what?"

"The dog."

"What dog?"

"On the side of the road . . . "

"Dead?"

"No. Abandoned."

"Hey, don't go getting so worked up about it."

"No, it's the way he looked at me, don't you see?"

They didn't see.

I am sure that dog was looking *at me*.

It made me sad as hell, and then Lola said something about our escape and she howled the music from *Mission Impossible* at the top of her lungs and I stopped thinking about the dog.

I sat there holding the map and daydreaming, thinking about those poker games from last night. I had really stuck my neck out, that last round with my four loser deuces, but what do you know . . . I had won all the same.

And now it all made sense.

W hen we got there, the last tour of the day had just started.
A young guy, white as an aspirin and pretty scruffy-looking, his gaze that of a cow in aspic, suggested we join the group up on the second floor.

There were a few wayward tourists, women with flabby thighs, indifferent families, grouchy kids, a pair of meditative schoolteachers in their Birkenstocks, and a handful of Hollanders. They all turned around and stared when we joined the group.
As for Vincent, he hadn't seen us yet. He had his back to us and was waffling on about his machicolations with a zeal we didn't know he had in him.

Initial shock: he was wearing a threadbare blazer, a striped shirt, cuff links, a little ascot in his collar, and a sketchy pair of pants, but with cuffs all the same. He was close-shaven and his hair was combed back.

Second shock: the complete and utter bullshit coming out of his mouth.

This château had been in the family for several generations. Nowadays, he lived there on his own while waiting to start a family and restore the moats.

The place had a curse on it because it had been built in secret for the mistress of François I's third bastard, a certain Isaure de Haut-Brébant who had gone mad with jealousy, so the legend went, and who dabbled in witchcraft when the fancy took her.

" . . . And even today, ladies and gentlemen, on nights when the moon is orange, during the first decan, you can hear very strange sounds, a sort of groaning, coming from the cellars, the very cellars that were used as a prison once upon a time . . .

"When my grandfather was in the process of remodeling the present-day kitchens, which you will see shortly, he discovered bones dating from the time of the Hundred Years' War, and a few écus stamped with the seal of Saint Louis. On your left is a tapestry from the twelfth century, and on your right, a portrait of the famous courtesan. Notice the beauty spot beneath her left eye, irrefutable proof of some sort of divine curse . . .

"Whatever you do don't miss the magnificent view from the terrace. On very windy days, you can just make out the towers of Saint-Roch . . .

"This way, please. Mind the step."

Pinch me, I must be dreaming.

The tourists stared attentively at the witch's beauty spot, and asked him whether he was ever afraid at night.

"By Jove, I have all I need to defend myself!"

With a broad swoop of his arm he took in armor, halberds, crossbows and other assorted clubs and bludgeons hanging in the stairway.

The visitors nodded gravely and cameras were raised.

What on earth was this utter lunacy?

When we walked by him as we left the room, his face lit up. Very discreetly, mind, a nod at most. The complicity of blood and long-standing affiliation.

The emblem of true nobility.

Amidst helmets and harquebuses we collapsed in laughter, while he went on to enumerate the difficulties inherent in the maintenance of such a demesne . . . Four hundred square meters of roofing, two kilometers of gutters, thirty rooms, fifty-two windows and twenty-five fireplaces, but— no heating. Or electricity for that matter. And no running water, now that you mention it. Whence the difficulty, for your humble servant, in finding a fiancée . . .

The visitors were laughing.

" . . . Here you have a very rare portrait of the Comte de Dunois. Notice the coat of arms, which you will also find sculpted on the pediment of the grand stairway in the northwest corner of the courtyard.

"We are now entering a bedroom with an alcove that was furnished in the eighteenth century by my ancestor the marquise de La Lariotine, who came fox hunting in the region. Not only for foxes, alas . . . And my poor uncle, the marquis, had no cause to be jealous of the magnificent stag antlers I am sure you paused to admire in the dining room earlier on the tour . . . Do be careful, Madame, that is frag-

ile. Now, I recommend you have a look in the little bathroom just here . . . The brushes, salt boxes and jars of oint-
ment are all original . . . No, mademoiselle, that chamber
pot is from the second half of the twentieth century and
that is a container for absorbing humidity . . .

" . . . Now we are coming to the most beautiful part of the
château, the spiral staircase of the north wing with its superb
annular barrel vault. A pure Renaissance masterpiece . . .

"Please don't touch—time is hard at work, and a thousand fingertips, I am sorry to say, can do all the damage of
one tiny miner's hammer . . . "

I could not believe my ears.

"Unfortunately I cannot show you the chapel, which is
presently under restoration, but I beg you not to leave my
modest dwelling until you have had a stroll through the
grounds, where you cannot help but feel the strange vibra-
tions coming from all these stones which, may I remind
you, were brought here for the purpose of providing a
refuge for the love of a man who was but a mere heartbeat
from the throne, and who had been cruelly caught in the
net of a wicked enchantress . . . "

Murmurs in the audience.

" . . . For those of you who are interested, near the exit
to the grounds you can have your picture taken in a suit of
armor, and that is also where you will find postcards and
the restrooms.

"I wish you all a pleasant day. May I remind you, ladies and gentlemen, please do not forget your guide. What am I saying—guide! A poor man indentured to his estate! A privileged slave, who asks not for alms but merely a means of subsistence, until the Comte de Paris is restored to his rightful throne . . .

"Thank you.

"Thank you, Mesdames.

"Dank u wel, Meneer . . . "

We followed the group; he disappeared through a secret door.

The yokels were beguiled.

We smoked a cigarette while we waited.

A guy at the entrance rigged the kids up in a dented suit of armor and took pictures of them while they brandished their weapon of choice.

Two Euros per Polaroid.

"Jordan, do be careful! You're going to poke your sister's eye out!"

Either this guy was way zen, or way stoned, or way retarded. He moved around very slowly and deliberately and seemed to have no nerves at all. With a super strong Gitane dangling from his lips and a Chicago Bulls baseball cap on backwards: it was disconcerting to watch him. *Fantasia* meets *Forrest Gump*, sort of.

"Jordan! Put that thing down!!"

Once everyone had left, Way Retarded took a rake and shuffled off, munching on his smoke.

We were beginning to wonder whether the little baron de La Lariotine would ever condescend to grace us with his presence . . .

I could not stop saying, "Pinch me . . . Can you believe this? . . . What the . . . " and shaking my head.

Simon became very engrossed in the mechanism of the drawbridge, and Lola set about rearranging a rambling rose.

Vincent emerged at last, with a smile. He was wearing a worn pair of jeans and a Sundyata T-shirt.

"Hey! What the fuck are you guys doing here?"

"We missed you . . . "

"Really? Awesome."

"How're things?"

"Great. Aren't you supposed to be at Hubert's wedding?"

"Yeah, but we got lost on the way."

"I see . . . cool."

That was him all over. Calm, kind. Not making a big deal out of seeing us there, but really happy all the same.

A moonstruck Pierrot, a Martian, our little brother, our very own Vincent.

It was cool.

"So," he said, spreading his arms, "what do you think of my little campground?"

"Yeah, what the hell do you mean bullshitting everyone like that?"

"What? You mean the stuff I tell people? Oh . . . it's not all bullshit. She really existed, this Isaure, it's just that . . . Well, I can't be sure she came through here . . . According to the archives, she's actually from the dump down the road

but since their château burned down, down the road . . .
We had to find her somewhere to live, no?"

"Yeah, but what about all that palaver, about ancestors
and dressing up like an impoverished toff, and all the fairy
tales you were telling them just now?"

"Oh, that? Put yourselves in my place. I got here beginning of May to work the season. The old biddy told me she
was going off on her spa treatment and she'd pay me the
first month when she got back. Since then, not a word.
She's vanished. It's already August and I haven't seen a
shekel. No lady of the manor, no pay stub or money order,
nada. I've got to live off something, no? That's why I had
to make up that whole shtick. All I've got to live on is the
tips, and you can't get tips just like that. People want their
money's worth and as you can see it's not exactly
Disneyland, here . . . So I get out the blazer and the signet
ring, and head straight for the battlements."

"Unbelievable."

"Ah, my good woman, you gotta do what you gotta do."

"And who's the other guy?"

"That's Nono. He gets paid by the village council."

"And uh, isn't he—does he have all his marbles?"

Vincent finished rolling his cigarette, then said, "I don't
really know. All I know is that he's Nono. If you understand Nono, that's fine, otherwise, it's hard going."

"But what do you do all day?"

"In the morning I sleep, in the afternoon I lead the
tours, and the evening is for my music."

"Here?"

"In the chapel. I'll show you. And what about you
guys? What are you up to?"

"Well, we, uh . . . not much. We wanted to take you out for dinner."

"When? Tonight?"

"Well, yeah, you dork. Not after the next Crusades."

"Nah, tonight's no good. Nono's niece is getting married, and I'm invited . . . "

"Hey . . . Just let us know if we're in the way, all right?"

"You're not, not at all! It's really great you're here. We'll work something out . . . Nono!"

Nono turned around, slowly.

"Do you think it would be at all a bother if my brother and sisters came along this evening?"

Nono stared at us for the longest time, then said, "He's your brother?"

"Yeah."

"And they're your sisters?"

"Yes."

"They still virgins?"

"Hey, Nono, that's not what I asked you! Shit, man . . . Do you think they can come tonight?"

"Who?"

"Oh, fuck, this guy's gonna drive me crazy—my brother and sisters!"

"Come where?"

"To Sandy's wedding!"

Nono pointed his chin toward me and said, "Will she be coming, too?"

Gulp.

Why do I get stuck with the horrible Gollum?

Vincent slumped in despair.

"He drives me crazy. Just recently, I don't know how he did it, there was this kid who got stuck in the suit of armor and we had to call the fire department . . . What are you laughing about? You're not the ones who have to deal with him every day, all right?"

"So why are you going to his niece's wedding, then?"

"I have no choice. He's really sensitive, you know. Yeah, yeah, go ahead and laugh, my lady virgins . . . Say, Simon, they haven't changed, these two, have they . . . Besides, his mother gives me loads of really good stuff. Terrines, vegetables from her garden, salami . . . If it weren't for her, I wouldn't survive."

I could not believe my ears.

"Anyway, this is all very well, but I've got to count up the money in the cash register, clean the toilets, help the dumbbell rake the walks, and lock all the doors."

"How many are there?"

"Eighty-four."

"We'll help."

"Hey, cool. There's a rake over there, and for the toilets, you take the hose."

We rolled up the sleeves of our fine apparel and got to work.

I think we're looking good. Do you want to go for a swim?"

"Where?"

"There's a stream, down there . . . "

"Is it clean?" asked Lola.

"You sure the foxes don't piss in it?" I added.

"Excuse me?"

We weren't too hot about the idea.

"Are you going?"

"I go every evening."

"Okay, we're coming."

Simon and Vincent were walking ahead.

"I have a vinyl of MC5 for you."

"No, really?"

"I do, yeah."

"First pressing?"

"Yup."

"Awesome. How did you find it?"

"Zounds, there is nothing too grand for our lord and master."

"You coming for a swim?'

"Of course."

"Hey, girls! You coming for a swim?"

"No way, not while that maniac is in the neighborhood," I murmured to Lola.

"No, we'll just watch!"

"He's around here somewhere," I muttered, clenching my teeth. "I can feel it. He's staring at us, from behind the bushes . . . "

My sister just laughed.

"Pinch me, I must be dreaming, I swear . . . "

"You already told us to pinch you, we got it. Go on, sit down."

Lola pulled the trashy magazine from my bag and looked up our horoscope.

"You're Aquarius, aren't you?"

"Huh? What?" I went, turning around abruptly to scare off Nono the onanist.

"Right . . . are you listening?"

"Yes."

"Be on your guard. Venus is in Leo, anything can happen. An encounter, True Love, the one you are waiting for is close at hand. Make the most of your charm and sex appeal and, above all, leave yourself open to chance. Your strong character has played tricks on you in the past. Time to indulge in some romantic sentiment."

She was killing herself laughing, the idiot.

"Nono! Come back! She's here! She wants to indulge in some roman—"

I put my hand over her mouth.

"Would you shut up? I'm sure you just made it all up."

"No way! Here, look if you don't believe me!"

I tore the rag from her hands.

"Show me—"

"There, look . . . *Venus is in Leo,* I'm not making it up."

"What absolute bullshit . . . "

"Well, if I were you, I'd be on my guard all the same."

"Tsk. This is all bullshit."

"You're right. Let's have a look and see who's been prancing around Saint-Tropez . . . "

"Hang on. No way you're going to tell me those are real tits?"

"Yeah, doesn't look like, does it?"

"And have you seen the . . . Eeeee! Simon, get the hell out or I'll call your wife!"

Like two dogs, the boys were shaking themselves gleefully, showering us with icy water.

We should have seen it coming . . . Or remembered, rather . . . Vincent had his cheeks full of water and started chasing after Lola, who ran screaming across the field, popping all the buttons off her dress.

I hurried to pick up all our things and went to join them, spitting at every bush I went by, making the sign of snail's horns with my index finger and pinkie.

Begone, Beelzebub!

Vincent took us on the tour of his private quarters in the servants' wing.

Basic.

He had brought a bed down from the second floor—where it was too warm for him—and made his niche in the stable. And what do you know, he'd chosen the box that had belonged to Lover Boy.

Between Polka and Hurricane . . .

He'd done himself up like a lord. Boots impeccably polished. A pure white 1970s suit. Hip-huggers and a pale pink silk shirt with a collar so pointy that it reached the armholes. On anyone else it would have looked ridiculous, but on Vincent it was as classy as it gets.

He went to grab his guitar. Simon took the wedding gift from the trunk of the car and we headed down to the village.

The evening light was sublime. The whole countryside was ochre, bronze, and old gold, resting from a long day. Vincent told us to turn around and admire his castle.

It was splendid.

"You're teasing me."

"Not at all, no way," said Lola, always mindful of Universal Harmony.

Simon began to sing, "I'm the king of the caaaastle, and you're the dirty raaaascals . . . "

Simon was singing, Vincent was laughing, and Lola was smiling. All four of us were walking along a warm pavement leading into a little village in the Indre.

There was a faint smell of tar, mint, and freshly mown hay in the air. The cows gazed at us admiringly and the birds called to each other, time for dinner.

A few grams of something sweet.

Lola and I had put our hats and various disguises back on.
No reason not to: a wedding is a wedding.

Or, at least that is what we figured, until we arrived at
our destination . . .

We entered an overheated parish hall that smelled of
sweat and old socks. Tatami mats were piled high in one
corner and the bride was sitting under a basketball hoop.
She looked as if she didn't know what hit her.

The tables were laid out for a banquet worthy of Astérix,
with local bag-in-box wine and music on full volume.

A huge lady all wrapped in ruffles hurried over to our
little brother.

"Ah! Here he is! Come here, son, follow me! Nono said
you had family with you. All of you, follow me, come on!
Just look at you all, you look grand! What a hat! And what
a slip of a girl this one is! You're so thin, don't they feed
you in Paris? Have a seat. Have something to eat, children.
Eat whatever you want. There's plenty. Just ask Gérard to
get you something to drink. Gérard! Come over here, lad!"

Vincent could not extricate himself from her hugs and
kisses; I stood there comparing. What a difference between
this woman, a complete stranger, and the polite disdain of my
great aunts just a few hours ago. I could not believe my eyes.

"Maybe we should go and congratulate the bride, don't
you think?"

"Go right ahead," said the huge lady, "and see if you
can't find Gérard on the way . . . Unless he's already under
the table, oh, that wouldn't look too good now."

"What's the present?" I asked Simon.
He didn't know.

We kissed the bride, one after the other.
The groom was as red as a lobster. He was looking skeptically at the gift his bride had just unwrapped: a superb cheese plate, carefully chosen by Carine. It was an oval thing with handles made of vine stock and vine leaves sculpted in the Plexiglas.
I don't think he was particularly impressed.

We sat down at the end of a table, and two old guys who were already pretty far gone welcomed us with open arms.
"Gé-rard! Gé-rard! Gé-rard! Hey, kids! Go get some food for our friends. Gérard! Where the hell did he get to?"
Gérard arrived with his bag-in-box and the party began.

After mixed veg in mayonnaise on a scallop shell, grilled lamb with French fries à la mayonnaise, goat cheese, and three slices of wedding cake, everyone moved back to make room for Guy Macroux and his *orchestre de charme.*

We felt blessed. Ears and eyes open wide. On our right was the bride, opening the dance with her dad, to an air by Strauss on the squeeze box, and to our left were the old guys, noisily crossing swords over the new one-way sign in front of the Pidoune bakery.
It was all so picturesque.
No. I can put it better than that, and less condescendingly: it was a moment to savor.

Guy Macroux had something of Dario Moreno about him.

Little dyed mustache, a flamboyant jacket, expensive bling, and a velvety voice.

With the first bars of the accordion, everyone flocked to the dance floor.

*"Pdum pdum pdum, just a little chachacha
Ah!
Pdum pdum pdum, step to the mambo
Oh!"*

"C'mon, all together now!"
La la la la . . . la la la la . . .
"I can't hear you!"
LA LA LA LA . . . LA LA LA LA . . .

"And in the back, there! Our grannies! Sing along, girls!"
Opidibi poi poi!

Lola and I went wild, and I had to roll up my skirt to keep the rhythm.

The boys, as usual, weren't dancing. Vincent was chatting up a young lady with a milky décolleté, and Simon was listening to some old timer's mildewed memories.

Then we had, *Gar-ter! Gar-ter! Gar-ter!* where things got a little steamed up and there was a lot of joking about big sausages. The young bride was wheelbarrowed onto a ping-pong table and . . . jeez, well, it's not really worth going into. Or maybe it's just me, maybe I'm too squeamish.

I went outside. I was beginning to miss Paris.

Lola came to join me for "ze moonlight cigarette."
This guy followed her out, his matted body hair gleaming with sweat. He just had to ask her to dance again.
He was wearing a Hawaiian shirt, viscose pants, white socks with a tennis stripe, and woven loafers.
Irresistibly charming.
And, and, and—I almost forgot: one of those black leather photographer's vests! Three pockets on the left and two on the right. And a penknife in his belt. And a cell phone in a case. And an earring. And dark glasses. And a chain attached to his wallet. All that was missing was the whip.
Indiana Jones in person.

"You gonna introduce me?"
"Uh, yes, this is my sister Garance, and uh—"
"You forgot my name already?"
"Uh . . . Jean-Pierre?"
"Michel."
"Oh, yes, Michel! Michel Garance, Garance Michel . . . "
"Hi," I said, as sternly as possible.
"Jean-Michel. My name is Jean-Michel . . . Jean like John and Michel like Mont-Saint-Michel, but hey, I won't hold it against you . . . Cheers! So you're sisters, huh? It's weird, you don't look at all alike . . . Are you sure one of you wasn't delivered with the mail?"
Ha. Ha. Ha.

Once he'd moved away, Lola shook her head.

"God, I couldn't take it anymore, how did I get stuck with the biggest creep in the county? Did you note his refined sense of humor . . . Even Comedy Central couldn't find him a slot. That guy is a disaster . . . "

"Shush, he's headed back this way."

"Hey! You heard the one about the guy with five dicks?"

"Uh . . . no. Haven't had that good fortune."

"So there's this guy. He's got five dicks."

Silence.

"So?" I ask.

"So his briefs fit him like a glove!"

Help.

"And the one about the whore who wouldn't suck dick?"

"Sorry?"

"You know what men call a whore who won't suck dick?"

More than anything, it was my sister's expression that made me want to laugh. My sister, always so classy with her vintage Saint Laurent, her refined ballet school gestures, her intaglio ring, and the way she could get all flustered just eating off a paper tablecloth . . . So with her flabbergasted air and her eyes big as Sèvres bisque saucers, it was glorious.

"Well?"

"Sorry, no. I give up, too. What do you call a call girl who, er—"

(Classy *and* funny. I adore her.)

"Well, they don't call her! Ha! Ha! Ha!"

He was on a roll, now . . . He swiveled around to face me, hanging by his thumbs from the pockets of his vest:

"And you? Have you heard the one about the guy who wrapped his hamster in duct tape?"

"No. But I don't want you to tell it because it's too disgusting."

"Oh, yeah? So you have heard it?"

"Uh, look, Jean-Montsaintmichel, I need to have a few words with my sister, here . . . "

"Okay, okay, I'll go. So, anyway, see ya later, pussycats!"

"Is he gone? Really truly gone?"

"Yes, but Toto is coming to take his place."

"Who's Toto?"

Nono sat down on a chair across from us.

He was looking at us, very diligently scratching the inside of his pants pockets.

Oh-kay.

Probably it was his brand-new suit; must have been causing him some local itching.

Saint Lola gave him a faint smile to put him at ease.

Of the type: Hiya Nono. We're your new friends! Welcome to our heart . . .

"Are you still virgins?" he asked.

Did he have a bee in his bonnet or what?! (No way!)

Our Singing Nun kept her cool: "So, it seems you're the caretaker over at the château?"

"Hey, you shut up. I'm talking to her, the one with the big tits."

I knew it. Yes, I knew it.

Someday we'll all laugh about it. Someday we'll be old and gray and since we won't have done our Kegel exercises the way we should, we'll piss our pants when we look back on this day. But at the time, it didn't make me laugh at all because . . . because Nono was drooling a little bit out of the side of his mouth that wasn't holding his cigarette butt, and it really spooked me. The thin thread of saliva just kept coming, in the moonlight . . .

Thank God, Simon and Vincent showed up just then.

"Shall we be off?"

"Good idea."

"I'll catch up with you, I just have to pick up my honorarium."

All the love I have for you-ou-ou
Wap doo wa dowa dowa . . . Wap doo wa . . .
Guy Macroux's voice echoed along the village streets. We danced our way through the parked cars.
My cries of joy-oy-oy, they're thanks to you-ou-ou

"Where are you taking us?"

Vincent was circling the château, heading down a dark path.

"Let's have one last drink. A nightcap if you wish. Are you tired, girls?"

"What about Nono? Is he following us?"

"Of course not. Forget about him. Are you coming?"

It was a gypsy camp. There were twenty caravans or so, each one bigger than the last and there were big white minivans, laundry, quilts, bicycles, kids, washbasins, tires, satellite dishes, TVs, cookpots, dogs, hens, and even a little black piglet.

Lola was horrified.

"It's after midnight and these kids aren't in bed. Poor things . . . "

Vincent laughed.

"Do you think they look unhappy or something?"

The kids were laughing, running all over the place; they rushed up to Vincent. They fought over who would carry his guitar and the little girls took us by the hand.

They were fascinated by my bangles.

"They're on their way to Saintes-Maries-de-la-Mer . . . I hope they'll be gone by the time the old biddy comes back, because I'm the one who told them they could stay here . . . "

"Just like Captain Haddock in *The Castafiore Emerald*," laughed Simon.

An old Rom took Vincent in his arms.

"Hey son, here you are."

He'd certainly found himself a few families, our little Vincent. It was hardly surprising he'd snubbed ours.

And then it was straight out of an old Kusturica film, from the time before he got bigheaded.

The old guys were singing these songs so sad you could weep, it just turned you inside out, and the young ones were clapping their hands while the women danced around the fire. Most of them were fat and badly dressed but when they moved, the very air around them seemed to be in motion.

The kids were still running all over the place and the grannies were watching television and rocking the babies to sleep. Almost all of them had gold teeth, and they smiled proudly to make sure we knew it.

Vincent was right at home with them, in hog heaven. He played his guitar: his eyes were closed, maybe just a fraction more concentrated than usual, so he could keep the tune and a certain distance.

The old men had fingernails like talons and the wood on the fret boards of their guitars was all worn down beneath the strings.

Gling, gling, toc.

Even if you didn't understand the words, it wouldn't be hard to guess the lyrics:

Where are you, my country? Oh where are you, my love?
Oh where are you, my friend? Oh where are you, my son?

And it went on to say, more or less,

I have no more country, only memories now.
My love is gone, only heartache now.
I've lost my friend, this song is for him.

An old woman brought us some flat beer. The minute we finished our glasses she came back with more.

Lola's eyes were shining; she was sitting with two kids on her lap, rubbing her chin on their hair. Simon looked at me with a smile.

We had come a long way, the two of us, since that morning . . .

Oops, here comes the irrepressible old granny with her lukewarm watery lager.

I motioned to Vincent to ask him if he had some smoke, but his answer was along the lines of hush, later. This was a new twist . . . Here we were among these good folk who don't send their kids to school, and there might well be a little Mozart rotting away in this dump of theirs, and they do what they like with the laws we hard-working sedentary folk come up with, but they don't smoke weed.

By all the saints of Merco-Benz, we'll have none of that here.

Y ou girls take Isaure's bed."
    "With all that moaning from the dungeon? No
    thanks."
"But that's just bullshit!"
"And with that dumbass who has a set of keys? No way.
We're sleeping in here with you!"
"All right, just chill, Garance."
"Don't tell me to chill! I am still a virgin, you better
believe it!"
I was dead tired, but I still managed to get a laugh out
of them. I was actually rather proud of myself.

The boys slept in Lover Boy's stall, and we curled up in
Hurricane's.

Simon woke us. He'd been down to the village for
croissants.
"From Pidoule's?" I asked with a yawn.
"From Pidoule's."

Vincent didn't open the gates that day.
"Closed due to rock fall," he wrote on a piece of cardboard.

He showed us around the chapel. He and Nono had moved the château's piano up to the altar so now all the angels in heaven could swing along.

We were treated to a little concert.

There we were, on a Sunday morning, sitting in a pew. Well-mannered and contemplative in the light of the stained glass, listening to "Knock Knock Knockin' on Heaven's Door " . . .

Lola wanted to visit every nook and cranny of the château. I asked Vincent to give us a rerun of his show. We were falling over each other laughing.

He showed us everything: the chatelaine's chambers, her girdles, her commode, her coypu traps, her recipes for coypu pâté, her bottle of hooch, and her old guide to the *Peerage, Baronetage & Knightage*, greasy from so much fingering. And then the cellars, the wines, the outbuildings, the saddle room, the hunting lodge and the old rampart walk.

Simon was amazed by the ingeniousness of the architects and other fortress-building experts. Lola was herb-gathering.

I sat down on a stone bench and observed the three of them.

My brothers leaning over the moat . . . Simon must be missing his latest remote-controlled model . . . Oh if only See-sull Dabbleyou were here . . . Vincent must have read his mind, because he said, "Forget about your little boats. There are humongous carps in there. They'd chew them up in no time."

"Are you serious?"

A dreamy silence, to stroke the lichen on the parapet . . .

"Actually, you know what?" murmured our Captain Ahab eventually, "it would be much more entertaining. I'll have to come back with Léo. Just to see some huge submoatian monster swallow down those precious toys he's never had the right to go near—might be the best thing that could ever happen to the two of us."

I didn't hear what he said after that but I could see they were high-fiving as if they'd just made a really good deal.

And there was my Lola, on her knees with her sketchbook among the daisies and the sweet peas . . . My sister's back, two daring white butterflies, her hair held up in a paintbrush, her long neck, her arms emaciated by a long divorce, the bottom of her T-shirt in a crumple as she used it to smudge her paint. A palette of white cotton that gradually took on its own colors . . .

I have never been more sorry not to have my camera with me.

Let's just chalk it up to fatigue, but I found myself wallowing in sentimentality. A huge wave of tenderness washed over me looking at the three of them: somehow this felt like the last magic show, the last birthday party of our childhood . . .

For almost thirty years they'd been making my life a place of beauty . . . What would I become without them? When would life decide it was time for us to part?

For that's the way it goes. For time parts those who love one another, and nothing lasts.

*

What we were experiencing at that moment—something all four of us were aware of—was a windfall. Borrowed time, an interlude, a moment of grace. A few hours stolen from other people . . .

For how much longer will we have the strength to tear ourselves away from everyday life and resist? How often will life give us the chance to play hooky? To thumb our noises at it? Or make our little honorarium on the side? When will we lose one another, and in what way will the ties be stretched beyond repair?

How much longer until we become too old?

And I know we were all aware of this. I know what we're like.

We were too shy to talk about it, but at that precise moment on our journey, we knew.

We knew that in the shadow of that ruined castle we were living the last hours of an era, and the time for change was drawing near. Time to part with closeness and tenderness, with our rough-and-tumble love for each other. Time to let go; open our palms and grow up, at last.

Time for the Dalton Gang to go their separate ways and ride off into the sunset . . .

I'm such a dork. I'd almost worked myself up into a state of solitary weeping when I saw something by the side of the path . . .

What was that thing?

I stood up, squinting.

An animal, a little creature was struggling to make its way toward me.

Was he hurt? What was it?

A fox?

A fox with his jar of urine, an emissary from Carine?

A rabbit?

It was a dog.

Unbelievable.

It was the dog I'd seen from the car yesterday, the one who'd dissolved in the rearview mirror . . .

It was the dog my eyes had locked gazes with, a hundred kilometers from here . . .

No. It couldn't be him. But I think it was . . .

Hey, at this rate, they'll want me on Animal Planet!

I knelt down and held out my hand. He didn't even have the strength left to wag his tail. He took three more steps and collapsed at my feet.

For a few seconds I didn't move. I was scared shitless. A dog had just come to die at my feet.

But then he gave a heartbreaking little whimper, trying to lick his paw. He was bleeding.

Lola came over and said, "Where'd this dog come from?"

I looked up at her and answered bleakly, "I cannot believe my eyes."

Now the four of us were on our knees to see what he needed. Vincent went to fetch some water, Lola to find some food, and Simon stole a cushion from the yellow salon.

The dog gulped down the water then collapsed in the dust. We carried him into the shade.

This business was downright weird.

We put together a picnic and went down to the river.

My throat was tight at the thought that the dog would probably be history by the time we came back up. But what could . . . At least he'd chosen a beautiful spot for it. And he'd have keeners as good as they come.

The boys wedged the bottles in the stones at the edge of the river while we spread a blanket. We had just sat down when Vincent said, "Hey look, there he is."

The dog dragged himself over to me once again. He curled up against my thigh and fell asleep at once.

"I think he's trying to tell you something," said Simon.

All three of them were laughing, teasing me: "Hey Garance, don't make such a face. He loves you, that's all. Come on . . . Say cheese. It's no big deal."

"But what the hell am I supposed to do with a dog? Can you see me in my tiny studio on the seventh floor with a dog?"

"There's nothing you can do about it," said Lola, "remember your horoscope? You've got Venus in Leo and you just have to accept it. This is the important encounter you had to prepare yourself for. I warned you . . . "

Another round of laughter.

"Consider it a sign from fate," said Simon, "this dog has come to save you—"

"—so that you'll lead a healthier, more balanced lifestyle—" added Lola.

"—and get up in the morning to take him out for a wee," said Simon. "You'll have to buy a tracksuit and take him jogging in the country every weekend."

"This way you'll schedule your day, and you'll feel responsible," Vincent chimed in.

I was flabbergasted.

"Not the tracksuit, spare me . . . "

Vincent uncorked a bottle and said, "And he's a cute little guy, too."

Damn it, who could argue with that? He had bald spots and fleas and scabs, he was scruffy and ragged and mongrelly, but he was cute all right.

"Seeing he's made this huge effort to find you, after all, you're not about to abandon him, now, I hope?"

I leaned over to look at him. He was pretty smelly, for one thing . . .

"Will you take him to the SPCA?"

"Hey! Why me? We found him all together, may I remind you!"

"Look!" shouted Lola, "He's smiling at you."

Fuck. He was, too. He'd turned over and he was wagging his tail, limply, and he raised his eyes to look at me.

Oh . . . Why? Why me? Would he even fit in the basket on my bike? And my concierge had it in for me, as it was . . .

And what does a dog eat?

And how long does it live?

And what about that little shovel for picking up the dog doo? And the retractable leash, and the inane conversations with all the neighbors out walking their mutts after the evening TV movie, fellow members of the pooper scooper brigade?

Heaven help us . . .

The Bourgueil was nicely chilled. We nibbled on some *rillons* and spread *rillettes* thick as pillows on our bread, and slowly savored some warm, sweet tomatoes, pyramids of ashy goat cheese, and orchard pears.

How good it felt. The water gurgling, the wind in the trees and the chatter of birds. The sun glistened on the river, shooting sparks here, vanishing there, bursting against the clouds or running along the riverbanks. My dog was dreaming about soft squelchy tarmac, grunting with happiness, and the flies pestered us.

We talked about the same things we'd talked about at the age of ten, fifteen, and twenty: the books we'd read, the films we'd seen, the music we'd heard, and the places we'd discovered. We talked about the Gallica online library and all the other treasures you could find on the Internet, and about the musicians we loved, and about the train or concert tickets or the time off we dreamt of treating ourselves to, and the exhibitions we were bound to miss, and our friends and the friends of our friends and the love stories we had—or hadn't—played a part in. Mostly hadn't, as it happened, and that's when we were at our best. At telling the stories, I mean. Stretched out in the grass, devoured by all sorts of little insects, we teased each other and mocked our own selves, writhing with laughter and sunburn be damned.

And then we talked about our parents. The way we

always did. About Mom and Pop. Their new lives. Their own love stories. And our future. In short, the everyday trifles and the handful of people that filled our lives.

It wasn't much, trifles to many people, and yet a boundless fortune.

Simon and Lola talked about their children. Getting on in school, mischief, the sentences they should have written down somewhere so as not to forget them. Vincent talked at length about his music: should he go on with it? Where? How? With whom? And how much could he allow himself to hope? I told them about my new roommate who, yes, was legal this time, and my job, and how I wasn't at all sure I was cut out for the bar. So many years spent studying and so little self-confidence at the other end; it was disconcerting.

Had I missed a vital turning point? Where had I slipped up? And was there someone waiting for me somewhere? The other three encouraged me and shook me up a bit so I pretended to go along with all their kind words.

Anyway, we all were a bit shaken up, and we were all pretending to go along.

Because wasn't life a bit of a bluff, after all?

When the stack is too short and there are chips missing. When you've been dealt a lousy hand and you can't keep up . . . That much we all agreed on, the four of us, with our grand dreams and our rents to be paid the fifth of every month.

So we opened another bottle: Dutch courage.

Vincent made us laugh with his latest sentimental fiasco.

"Hey, put yourselves in my shoes! There's this girl I've been after for two months, I wait for her for six hours outside her department at the university, then I invite her out to eat, three times, and take her back to her student dorm in the middle of nowhere a dozen times, and I invite her to the opera, a hundred and ten Euros a shot! Shit!"

"And nothing's happened?"

"Nothing. Nada. Diddly squat. Shit! Two hundred and twenty Euros! Can you imagine how many records I could have bought with that?"

"Well, I might point out that a guy who nickels and dimes like that deserves what he gets," scolded Lola.

"But did you—did you even try and kiss her?" I asked naively.

"No. I didn't dare. That's what sucks, man."

Catcalls of the most eloquent variety.

"I know. I'm shy, it's stupid . . . "

"What's her name?"

"Eva."

"Where's she from?"

"Dunno. She told me, but I didn't understand."

"I see. And, uh . . . do you think you have a chance, or not?"

"Hard to say. But she showed me photos of her mother . . . "

Too much.

We rolled around in the grass while Don Juan tried to pelt us with pebbles.

"Oh," I begged, "can I have that one?"

Lola tore a page out of her sketchbook and handed it to me, rolling her eyes skyward.

She at least had been able to see the true nobility of that heroic mutt of mine as he languished in the sun. The only male, now that I think of it, who has ever pursued me with such constancy . . .

The next drawing was a very pretty view of the château.

"From the English garden," nodded Vincent.

"We should send it to Pop and write a little note," suggested Lola.

(Our Pop didn't have a cell phone. Come to think of it, he never had a landline either . . .)

Like all her other ideas from time immemorial, it was a good one, and as always and for all time, we fell in behind our elder sister.

It was as if we were at the back of the bus on our way home from summer camp. Paper and pen going from hand to hand. Thoughts, greetings, tenderness, mischief, little hearts and the big kisses that went with them.

The glitch—but that wasn't our Pop's fault, it was the fault of May '68—was that we didn't exactly know where to send our letter.

"I think he's working at a naval shipyard in Brighton . . . "

"Hardly," joked Vincent, "it's too cold for him there! He's got rheumatism these days, after all, the old geezer! He's in Valence with Richard Lodge."

"Are you sure?" I was surprised. "The last time I heard from him he was on his way to Marseille . . . "

Silence.

"Okay," decided Lola, "I'll keep it in my bag for now and the first one to hear something gets in touch with me."

Silence.

But Vincent strummed a few chords so that we would not hear it.

In her bag . . .

All those kisses, still stifled. All those hearts locked up along with keys and checkbooks.

But under all those cobblestones they'd hurled in youthful rebellion, there was nothing.

Luckily for me, I had my dog. He was covered with fleas and was conscientiously licking his goolies.

"Why are you smiling, Garance?" asked Simon, to conceal the moment of sadness.

"Nothing. Just thinking how lucky I am . . . "

My sister got her paints back out, the boys had a swim and I watched my sweetheart gradually come back to life as I handed him pieces of bread smeared with *rillettes*.

He spat the bread back out, the filthy cur.

"What are you going to call him?"

"I don't know."

Lola was the one who called time to leave. She didn't want to be late because of the transfer of custody, and you could tell she was already getting antsy. Worse than antsy, in fact: worried, brittle, her smile gone all crooked.

Vincent gave me back my iPod that he'd nicked months earlier.

"Here you go, like I promised ages ago, I've downloaded all the—"

"Oh, thanks! You put all the stuff I like?"

"No. Not everything, how could I. But you'll see, it's a good selection."

We all indulged in a few hugs, interspersed with idiotic jibes so we wouldn't get carried away, and then we went to lock ourselves away in the car. Simon had already driven across the moat before he slowed down. I leaned out the window to shout, "Hey! Lover Boy!"

"What?"

"I've got a present for you, too!"

"What is it?"

"Eva!"

"What d'you mean, Eva?"

"She's arriving day after tomorrow on the bus from Tours."

He was running after us.

"Huh? You're bullshitting me!"

"I'm not! We called her a while ago while you were swimming."

"Liars." (He was white as a sheet.) "How did you get her number, for a start?"

"We looked in the contacts on your cell."

"It's not true."

"You're right. It's not true. But go to the bus stop anyway, just in case."

He was all red.

"What the hell did you tell her?"

"That you live in a huge château and that you've written a beautiful solo for her and she has to hear it because you'd play it for her in a chapel and it would be really *romantichno* . . . "

"What the hell?"

"It's Serbo-Croatian."

"I don't believe you."

"Too bad for you, then. Let Nono take care of her."

"Is it true, Simon?"

"I have no idea, but knowing these two harpies, anything is possible."

He was bright pink.

"Are you serious? Day after tomorrow?"

Simon started the car again.

"The bus at 6:40 P.M.!" said Lola.

"Across from Pidoule's!" I shouted, over her shoulder.

When he had completely disappeared from the rear view mirror, Simon said, "Garance?"

"What?"

"Pidou-ne."

"Oh yeah, sorry. Look, there's that pervert! Squash him!"

We were going to wait until we were on the freeway to listen to Vincent's present.

Lola decided at last to ask Simon whether he was happy.

"Are you asking me because of Carine?"

"Sort of . . . "

"You know . . . She's much nicer at home. It's when you guys are around that she's a pain. I think she's jealous. She's afraid of you. She thinks I love you more than her and . . . and then, you stand for everything she is not. Your crazy side completely throws her. That *demoiselles de Rochefort* side. She's got her hang-ups. She's got the impression that for you two life is like some huge schoolyard and you're the popular girls who used to tease her because she was first in the class. Those beautiful, inseparable, funny of girls whom she secretly admired."

"If she only knew . . . " said Lola, putting her head against the window.

"But that's the thing, she doesn't know. When she's around you she feels completely lost. I know she can be a pain, but it's a good thing I have her . . . She encourages me, motivates me, she forces me to do things. Without her I'd still be in my curves and equations, that's a fact. Without her I'd be in some maid's room somewhere ruminating about quantum mechanics!"

He fell silent.

"And she has given me two beautiful gifts, after all . . . "

As soon as we'd gone through the tollbooth, I plugged the iPod into the car radio.

"So, buddy, what have you got for us, here?"

Trusting smiles. Simon tugged on his seatbelt to leave some room for the musicians. Lola reclined her seat and I nestled up against her shoulder.

Marvin as ringleader: *Here my dear . . . This album is dedicated to you . . .* A wild version of Miriam Makeba's "Pata Pata", to loosen our joints; "Hungry Heart" by the Boss because we'd been shaking our booties for fifteen years to that one; and further along on the playlist, "The River", to feed our hungry hearts. Then "Beat It" by the defunct Bambi, on full volume just long enough to slalom between the white lines. "Friday I'm in Love" by The Cure in order to—hang on, let me turn the sound down— greet this fine weekend; "Common People" by Pulp, a song that taught us more English than all our teachers put together. Then there was Boby Lapointe bemoaning the fact that *you're prettier than ever . . . except your heart.*

Your heart has lost that warmth I loved . . . A sublime version of "I Will Survive" by Musica Nuda and a completely cracked version of "My Funny Valentine" by Angela McCluskey. And then another one of hers, "Don't Explain", enough to make the most hardened womanizer weep. Yo-Yo Ma's cello for Ennio Morricone and his Jesuits. Dylan saying over and over *I want you* to two sisters who are practically virgins. *Love me or leave me,* begs Nina Simone, and I'm surprised to see Lola rubbing her nose . . . Vincent doesn't like to see his sister unhappy so he forwards to a penny whistle number from Riverdance to cheer her up. Björk wailing that it's too calm; Vivaldi's "Nisi Dominus" for Camille's sake, and the Neil Hannon song that Mathilde was crazy about. Kathleen Ferrier for Mahler, Glenn Gould for Bach, and Rostropovich for peace. Music from the film *Mamma Mia!* coming along just when I wasn't sure I wanted to hang around too much longer. Then a pause for the weather report, with "Stormy Weather" and then Luis Mariano yodeling about the sun in Mexico. Pyeng Threadgill sang "Close to Me"*,* and I said to myself, that's it exactly, my darlings. Cole Porter's elegance made even more sublime by Ella Fitzgerald, then some Cyndi Lauper for contrast. *Oh daddy! Girls just wanna have fu-un!* I shout, shaking my dog like a cheerleader's pompom, and all his fleas start dancing the Macarena.

And so many others. Megabytes to bliss out on.

Nods to the past and memories, all those greasy slow tracks in memory of rotten parties, *music was my first looove* (for connoisseurs only!), Klezmer, Motown, old dance-hall stuff, Gregorian chants, marching bands and grand organs and then suddenly, while the tank was gulping and the pump clicked madly, Léo Ferré and Louis Aragon sang out in protest, *Is this how man lives?*

The more tracks I heard, the harder it was to hold back my tears. Sure, I was tired, but I could feel this knot growing and growing at the back of my throat.

Too much emotion all at once. Simon and Lola and Vincent and Pinchme on my lap and all this music that had been my life support for so long . . .

I had to blow my nose.

When the iPod fell silent I thought I'd feel better, but then that bastard Vincent's voice came on through the loudspeakers.

"That's it. That's all for now, Gary. Anyway, I hope I haven't forgotten anything . . . Hang on, yes, here's one for the road."

Jeff Buckley's cover of Leonard Cohen's *Hallelujah.*

With the first notes of the guitar I bit my lips and stared at the overhead lamp to hold back my tears.

Simon adjusted his rearview mirror and immobilized me.

"You okay? Are you sad?"

"No," I replied, cracking at the seams, "I'm just really . . . really happy."

We spent the rest of the drive in complete and total silence. Rewinding the film and thinking about tomorrow.

Recess over. The bell was about to ring. Get in line, two by two.

Silence, please.
Silence, I said!

We dropped Lola off at the Porte d'Orléans and Simon drove me home and stopped right outside my door.

Just as he was about to pull away I put my hand on his arm: "Wait here, it'll only take a minute."

I rushed over to Monsieur Rashid's.

"Here," I said, handing Simon the packet of rice, "don't go forgetting the shopping."

He smiled.

He kept his arm raised for a long time, then once he had turned the corner I went back over to my favorite grocer's and bought some dog biscuits, and a can of Happychow.

"Garance, I warning you, your dog piss one more time on my eggplants, I gonna make meatballs outa him!"

ABOUT THE AUTHOR

Born in Paris in 1970, Anna Gavalda
published her first work in 1999 while
working as a high-school French teacher,
the critically acclaimed collection of
short stories *I Wish Someone Were
Waiting for Me Somewhere*, which sold
over half a million copies in her native'
France and was published in the US by
Penguin in 2003. Gavalda has since
published three novels, all of which have
become bestsellers across Europe. Her
first novel, *Someone I Loved*, was
adapted to film in 2009, and the film
adaptation of her novel *Hunting and
Gathering* starred Audrey Tautou and
Daniel Auteuil. Gavalda's novels and
short stories have been translated into
over forty languages. She lives in Paris.